AND ROUND ME RINGS

BELL TALES AND FOLKLORE

ANN SPENCER

ILLUSTRATED BY

LINDSAY GRATER

Tundra Books

Text copyright © 2003 by Ann Spencer
Illustrations copyright © 2003 by Lindsay Grater

Published in Canada by Tundra Books,
481 University Avenue, Toronto, Ontario M5G 2E9

Published in the United States by Tundra Books of Northern New York,
P.O. Box 1030, Plattsburgh, New York 12901

Library of Congress Control Number: 2003100908

National Library of Canada Cataloguing in Publication

Spencer, Ann, 1955-
And round me rings : bell tales and folklore / Ann Spencer ;
illustrated by Lindsay Grater.

ISBN 0-88776-597-1

1. Bells–Folklore. 2. Tales. I. Grater, Lindsay, 1952- II. Title.

PS8587.P317A75 2003   j398.27   C2003-900697-2
PZ8.1.S74An 2003

We acknowledge the financial support of the Government of Canada
through the Book Publishing Industry Development Program (BPIDP)
and that of the Government of Ontario through the Ontario Media
Development Corporation's Ontario Book Initiative. We further
acknowledge the support of the Canada Council for the Arts and the
Ontario Arts Council for our publishing program.

Although folktales and folk songs are by their very nature oral traditions,
every reasonable effort has been made to locate and acknowledge the
owners of copyright material in this volume. Any information about errors
or omissions would be welcomed by the publisher.

Design: Terri Nimmo

Printed and bound in Canada

1 2 3 4 5 6   08 07 06 05 04 03

For my mother, Marilyn Spencer,
with warm memories of our
family music-making evenings around
the piano. She made music
my second language and opened my ears
to the sweet sounds all around.
My life is richer for it.
A.S.

For Christopher, with love.
L.G.

AUTHOR'S NOTE

In 1996 I sat up in the ringing chamber of the Cathedral Church of the Holy Trinity in Quebec City. A chance meeting with bellringers on the streets below led to this unusual invitation. For four hours I listened to bell-ringing by members of the North American Guild of Change Ringers. The afternoon was interspersed with storytelling about bells, ringers, and belfries.

Ever since that afternoon high above Quebec City, I have listened differently to bells. I thought about all the bells of my childhood – the chimes at St. John's Anglican Church in Lunenburg, Nova Scotia and the summer serenades that ringer Edison Tanner played on the bells. Their sound wafted over the whole town. The old church burned down in the autumn of 2001, but those chimes are part of Lunenburg's fabric, as if their sounds still hang somewhere in the air, along with the old school and harbor bells.

This is the power of bells. They resonate deep within us as they play through the events of our lives and vibrate long afterward.

Prosperity to those who love bells.
– English bell inscription, 1718

CONTENTS

AND ROUND
ME RINGS

A cascade of silver
Singing the celebrations
Of newborns and brides
Feasts and glories.
And round me rings JOY.

A clash of metal
Blaring out doom
Of battles and murder
Attack and war.
And round me rings FEAR.

A lament of copper
Tolling out death
Of royals and peasants

Disasters and famine.
And round me rings SORROW.

A cry from steeples
Shrieking out warning
Of fire and flood
Storm and plague.
And round me rings PANIC.

A clang from towers
Signaling order
Of kingdoms and towns
Precision and justice.
And round me rings REASON.

A peal from rooftops
Resounding jubilations
Of victory and truce
Gratitude and freedom.
And round me rings PEACE.

Marking our days
Echoing through time
Our prayers, joys, and glories
Our heights and our depths.
And round me rings LIFE.

I

LET HEAVEN AND NATURE RING: ELEMENTAL PEALS

THE SUNKEN
CATHEDRAL

*Far out to sea, somewhere in the mist, the deep tolling of a
church bell and the chanting of monks can be heard, cush-
ioned by the ocean's roar. People, walking the rocky shore
and cliffs along the coast of Brittany, look out across the
bay. "Listen," they whisper, "the bells of Ys are tolling their
warning," and they fix their stares toward the veiled
horizon. For Breton legend tells that every one hundred
years, the sunken cathedral will rise from the sea and the
bells of Ys will ring out their watery peal.*

The cliffs had not always marked land's end in
Brittany. At one time they had been inland, sepa-
rated from the sea by the magnificent walled city
of Ys. King Gradon had built the city for his
golden-haired daughter, Dahut. The king knew his daughter

needed the sea to be nearby always, for Dahut had been born on the ocean and rocked to sleep by the gentle waves lapping against the royal boat. She loved the sea and could not sleep unless she heard the surf pounding nearby.

So King Gradon instructed his workers to build a city for the princess as near to the sea as possible. First they constructed an enormous seawall to stop the water from crashing in. Then they built the glorious city of Ys to the king's specifications. When all was ready and the tide was low, King Gradon, Princess Dahut, and all their subjects moved, in a long procession, down to their new city.

As soon as they entered, the king explained that although he had built Ys below sea level, they would always be safe. He showed them a large gold door built into one of the walls. "I, alone, have the key to this door. It shall be opened only when the seawater is low, and locked as soon as the tide bell rings. When the door is closed, no one may go in or out of the city."

The city of Ys flourished for many years. Dahut often ran along the seawall, looking out at the sparkling blue and green ocean. She loved the familiar lull of waves lapping just outside the castle wall. But the sea winds also whispered strange mysteries to her, revealing ancient secrets of dark and powerful magic. She was wild and bewitching, and many a man sought her hand in marriage. Dahut wanted no husband, until one day a stranger sailed up to the walled city of Ys.

He was dressed like a knight in a cloak of crimson, and Dahut was enchanted by his easy charm. She was so smitten, she did not sense the danger and darkness lurking in his words. The sound of his voice comforted her as only the ocean had ever been able to do. The knight asked her to unlock the gold door to the city, that he might come and go whenever she wished him. "You do not understand," Dahut protested, "only my father has the key."

The stranger smirked, although Dahut thought he smiled. "If indeed you love me as you say, Dahut," he said, "you will find it no problem to get the key. If you refuse, I will know you have been false in your words to me and I shall leave and never return." Dahut was in anguish, for she had been warned from little up never to open the gold door, but when she looked at the knight, she could not bear the thought of never seeing his beautiful face again.

"Wait here," she said. Dahut crept through the castle halls to the room where her father was sleeping. She tiptoed, ever so silently, across the cold stone floor to where her father's coat was set out. She fingered through the pockets until she grasped the key. Then she left the bedchamber and raced down to meet her knight.

"Go then, unlock the door," he ordered. Dahut trembled at the thought, but so fearful was she of losing the man she loved that she moved toward the gold door. She fitted the key into the lock and gave it a hard turn. Immediately there was a *thump* outside the door. She turned the gold handle and as soon as the door opened, a large wave bounded into the city. Dahut struggled to push the door closed, but the power of the sea was too great.

"Help me," she cried out to her knight. But his reply horrified her. The voice that had been so lulling and gentle was suddenly a powerful roar: "I am Ocean, you fool. For years I have been wanting to break down the walls of Ys, and now you have helped me." She watched in disbelief as he became part of the sea. His thunderous laugh and the pounding surf were now one.

Frantic, the princess ran to her father to wake him. "Father, the seawall has failed us and the water is coming in!" By now, the whole city was alerted to the flood by the great clanging coming from the cathedral towers.

"We must escape now, Dahut," the king cried. "There is but one way." They ran to the royal stables and King Gradon readied his black steed, Morvarc'h, for the journey. The powers of Morvarc'h were legendary, for the magnificent horse belonged to the sea. He had been a gift from the powerful queen of the North many years before King Gradon founded Ys.

The king and the princess mounted Morvarc'h and raced toward the door of the city. Already the water was rising and people were frenzied in the streets. As they were about to pass through the door, Morvarc'h came to an abrupt halt. There in front of them, barely discernible in the mist, was a ghostly figure draped in dark cloth. The specter lifted its thin finger and pointed to the princess: "You are the cause of your city's misfortune. Shame and disgrace have you brought to your people, for had you not stolen the key, all would be safe."

"Father, save me!" Dahut pleaded, as the waves rushed in around her feet. King Gradon motioned his horse to move, but Morvarc'h could not raise a hoof. The specter continued the story of Dahut's shameful actions, and King Gradon remained to hear how his beloved daughter had betrayed not only him, but also all of her subjects. He looked about as the sea swept over screaming women and their children. The king's fury rose. He pushed Dahut from the saddle into the sea. Then he commanded his horse to move, and Morvarc'h galloped over the water toward safety. A huge wave swelled behind them and the powerful seawater rushed toward the door of the city. Within seconds of the king's flight, all of Ys was engulfed in water. Every man, woman, and child drowned.

Tales of the glories of Ys continued through the centuries, and people dreamed of creating another magnificent city. The lovely French city of Lutece was renamed Paris, or Par Ys, which in Breton means 'like Ys.' The legend of Ys ends with a prophecy:

When Paris is engulfed by seas
Will reemerge the city of Ys.

As for Dahut, she became a mermaid. She swims through the seawater, where her proud city once stood. Sailors who have seen the golden-haired mermaid tell of the strange song she sings:

A siren Dahut will be
Til Ys rises from the sea.

BELL-DESPISING
FAERIES

Neither sleep, neither lie,
For Inkbro's ting-tangs hang so high.
– From *Aubrey's Miscellanies*
by John Aubrey

L ong ago, in the countryside of England, not far from Stratford-upon-Avon, faery folk and man dwelt peaceably alongside one another. The human world, in that part of the country, only glimpsed on the world of faery. It might have been a shimmer of sunlight that danced a little too long in the shadows, or a sudden wild breeze that seemed to blow up out of nowhere to send hats flying off heads. "Just faeries playing their little pranks. Harmless, really, dearies," mothers would tell their children as they tied up the little ones' bonnet strings. "Only do be careful never to anger the faery folk."

As for that countryside faery world, life with humans was uneventful enough. There was only one human habit that irritated faery folk, and that was incessant bell ringing. The church bells of Inkberrow rang for a great long time each and every morning. Now, faeries are light sleepers and the morning bells were most bothersome, especially when there had been much merriment around the toadstool the midnight hour before. The one comfort to the wee folk was that the bells of Inkberrow were over a mile away from their orchards, groves, and meadows.

But on a fine sunny day, just after the celebration of Midsummer's Eve, one tired faery awoke first to the distant bells and the sound of humans talking. Two children were playing near the faery's bird's nest bed. "My father says soon we won't have to strain so hard to hear the church bells ringing," one child told the other, "for they are going to tear down the old church and move it out to this great meadow."

"Good, then we won't have so far to walk to church," replied the other child. "But how does your father know this?"

"Because," answered the friend, "my father is a stone-mason and he is planning all the work. He says it is to be bigger than the old church and have more bells."

At this news, the faery bolted up in his nest and hissed. The children, thinking it was a great snake, for indeed the hiss was that loud, ran off home, screaming, "Snakes in the grove, beware! Snakes in the grove! Stay away!"

Of course, the faery couldn't help but snicker with glee for a second or two. It was splendid faery fun to play pranks on mortals, but then he recalled it was not intended to be a prank. He was upset at the shocking things the children were saying. "More bells," he yelled out the announcement, "more bells are coming and they will be right here in our grove." Faeries and their wild herds of cattle hastened to the tree where the nest was now shaking on the branch, so upset was its occupant.

"We will never sleep now," screamed the faery, who was shaking with such rage that he dislodged the nest and spilled out onto a leafy branch below. "*Ting Tang, Ding Dong*, all day long," he screamed again, and a bunch of acorns showered to the ground. The crowd below ran for cover under dandelions and toadstools. Then came a gentle ring of bluebells and the soft trumpeting of a morning glory to announce the approach of the faery queen. Faeries scrambled from treetops, rocks, and shelters to greet her.

The faery queen spoke: "The church must not be built in our grove. For the bells will end our peaceful mornings. Each one of you, my subjects, shall look to find ways to baffle these mortals as they try to work. Trip them up; cast a spell, if need be. Do whatever faery pranks you must to discourage and disrupt their plans. Now, be off like the wind, all of you. Fool and upset them all in the twinkling of an eye, so not one is aware such quicksilver folly be our handiwork."

And so it was that when the workers arrived the following day, strange things began to happen. One man, pacing across the meadow to measure the distance for digging, was caught unawares when a mischievous faery spell caused the grass to grab at his heels and wrap tightly around his ankles. In a flash, he was pulled to the ground. The poor man tried to get up, but he was bound by a strong unseen force. He cried out, but no one around seemed to hear his plea for help. Then hundreds of tiny hands reached up and pinched the worker. When his agony finally ended, the worker shouted once more. This time the entire work crew came running. He told his story. All looked at him in astonishment, for sure enough, his body was pinched black and blue.

After lunch, the foreman's wife strolled by with the couple's son in a pram. As soon as she neared the grove, a pram wheel came loose and the babe was jolted awake. But no one knew the true reason the son was screaming. When the babe looked up, he saw his mother surrounded by faery faces, all jeering and sticking their tongues out at him.

Still, the workers forged ahead and within the week they were ready to start building. The faeries made all manner of protest. Several of the masons thought they heard high-pitched whining sounds that made no sense to them at all. The faeries sent strong gusts of wind, but the workers only secured the bricks with extra mortar. No faery spell could budge the crew's resolve.

Finally the faery folk called a meeting to discuss the problem of the bells. They met in a ring and began a furious dance to commence the proceedings. A mason, who had stayed behind to have a short sleep before heading back to the village, awoke to a flurry of whirring and humming. He rolled over on his stomach and looked down from where he had been sleeping, over the small bank to a patch of grass by a moat below. He could hardly believe his eyes. The whirring noise was caused by the wild dance of a faery circle. He had heard of such creatures, but had never before seen them. After the dance they stopped, and the mason watched in amazement as a golden light descended on the tallest goldenrod. Then, in a flash, there appeared a most beautiful little faery woman, garbed in glittering gold. She wore a crown, and he knew it was the faery queen herself. He strained his ears to listen. At first he heard only high-pitched whisperings, much like the sound the wind makes when it blows through the treetops. Then from the sibilance came distinct sounds. *Ting Tang*, he heard, and *Ding Dong*.

Suddenly a trumpet blew and saucy voices cried out: "There be a mortal among us. He has invaded our faery privacy. A spell together we shall now cast." There was great muttering, like the low moaning of a wind. The mason tried to get up and run, but he could not. Milk thistles blew over him, tickling and making him dozy. Burrs and prickle bushes shot up all about him, pinning him to the ground. The day was strangely lazy and the sunlight itself seemed to kiss his eyes shut. Soon he was fast asleep.

The faeries gathered all about the sleeping man. "Now is the time for us to leave Inkberrow. These mortals and their despicable bells will change our faery ways. Therefore we leave this grove tonight, never to return." The faery queen looked one last time at their grove, and in a rainbow flash she was gone.

The faeries disappeared one by one throughout the evening, until only the most prankish of the group remained. He danced a jig on the sleeping mason, tickled him under the nose with a piece of grass, and leaped to a tree branch to shake acorns loose upon him. He pinched the poor fellow, then sang a great lament in the man's left ear. In a twinkling, the wild faery vanished.

The next morning, the other workers found their sleeping comrade beneath the oak tree. He was snoring loudly, covered with a dusting of milk thistle. All about him were acorns and blades of grass. "Whatever has old Thomas been up to all night?" asked one of his friends. He shook the man.

"*Ting Tang* and *Ding Dong*," old Thomas shouted out.

"What the heck is he talking about?" they said, and shook him a little harder.

"Hey, stop that," he yelled at them, "I'm sore all over. Why have you been pinching me all night long? I must be black and blue from all your foolishness." He lifted up his shirt, and indeed he was covered with hundreds of small bruises.

"But we've only just arrived," said the foreman. "Just as you were calling out something about *Ting Tang* and *Ding Dong*."

The mason scratched his head. "Why does that sound so familiar?" He thought long and hard, trying to piece together some faraway dream that somehow felt very real. He looked at his bruised arm and gasped, "Faeries – that's what I saw, then. Now what did they say?"

And he closed his eyes and thought the night over again. Suddenly he recalled the trick-playing faery's high-pitched voice. "Our bells drove them away!" he told the astonished workers. Then, as if in a trance, he delivered the message – the faery's parting lament – which had been spoken in his left ear. True to faery form, it was a message in rhyme:

> *Neither sleep, neither lie,*
> *For Inkbro's ting-tangs hang so high.*
> *Ting Tang, Ding Dong*
> *So long!*

WHITE CORAL BELLS

White coral bells upon a slender stalk,
Lilies of the valley deck my garden walk.
Oh, don't you wish that you could hear them ring?
That can happen only when the faeries sing.
                – Traditional round

BELLING
THE CAT

– An Aesop's Fable retold

Once, long ago, the mice held a special meeting to deal with the great problem of the house cat. It was a matter of survival as this cat was a vicious mouser. The mice decided it was time to devise a plan of action – one to keep themselves safe from attack. Suggestions were put forth from the floor, given consideration, debated, then voted on. Not one of the ideas could the mice agree upon.

"Alas, that cat is just too big and quick," a lady mouse sighed. The other mice nodded in agreement.

"If only we could hear him coming," lamented another with a bent ear, having once gotten too close to the cat's powerful paw.

"Now here's an idea," spoke up an old gray mouse of distinguished standing. The other mice listened closely as he continued: "I believe I have just the plan to deal with that treacherous feline. This solution will allow us to move with greater ease and safety through the house. Imagine," he whispered, "just imagine if we could hear the cat before he strikes. Then we could run."

"But the cat stalks us," said a mother mouse insistently. "I tell you, when my little ones are scuttering along, that cat walks as if his paws are padded with cotton. Oh, really, whatever can we do?" The mother mouse dissolved into a fit of tears.

"Madam," said the old gray mouse, "what if the cat had a bell fastened around his neck? It would not matter then how light or velvety his paws might be. Whenever he moves, we'd hear him tinkling and jingling."

There was great cheering and applause, and the suggestion was put to a vote. The mice decided to follow this plan, and began to chatter and squeak to one another about how great it would be to finally have warning of the cat's approach.

Then the oldest of those assembled spoke up: "Do excuse me, one and all. Let me say I agree wholeheartedly with each and every one of you that it is a marvelous idea to have warning of attack, but I must ask you: tell me, who is going to bell the cat?"

It is easy to propose impossible remedies.

THE GHOSTLY
FLOOD BELL

England's greatest flood of the 19th century was in 1875. The River Trent had risen to dangerous levels and was overflowing, spilling into towns and villages. In one small village, the streets were completely flooded by the sudden high waters. Villagers were stranded in the upstairs rooms of their houses and cottages. They were distressed by the chaos, worrying how far the waters would continue to rise. If the waters did not stop soon, they could only hope a boat was on its way to rescue them.

Nighttime was the worst. In the pitch dark, people's imaginations worked overtime. Well after midnight of the second night of their ordeal, the villagers opened their windows wide, amazed at the sound piercing the eerie darkness. From far off, a church bell was tolling.

"That's the bell from the church on the hill. But who could be ringing it?" yelled a man to his neighbor stranded across the way.

"Perhaps it is a warning bell," came the answer.

"No, listen closely," shouted another, "that is not a ring for danger. It is neither constant nor quick. There is no purpose to that ring."

The strange unmetered tolling continued all through the night. One old woman shrieked from her window, "The Lord be with us all, I swear there is a ghost ringing that bell. Perhaps it is tolling the death knell for every one of us." At this she became hysterical, and the night air filled with her wails and the eerie ringing of the church bell.

The bell continued to ring sporadically throughout the next day and night. It rang in the dawn of the fourth day. That morning the tired villagers were finally convinced the flood waters had subsided enough for them to leave safely, by rowboat, for supplies. As they set out in groups, the bell began to clang wildly, again with no sense of timing to the rings. A huge ring would sound out, followed by five minutes of silence, then a wobbly uncertain ring, as if someone was shaking the rope unable to decide whether to let the bell be heard.

"It sounds like the ringer is drunk," said the head rower of the group. "I think it's time we put a stop to this drunkard, or ghost, or whoever the blazes is ringing that bell."

They rowed to a point just below the church hillside. There they were able to leave their boat and walk up to the church, as the knoll was high enough to stay dry. But in the mud below the hill, they saw hoofprints. One villager crossed herself and cried: "Perhaps it is the devil himself ringing that bell."

The villagers entered the church hallway. Still the bell rang. The door to the ringing chamber was wide open and the mayor told them he would investigate the matter, moving toward the door. The villagers stood still, prepared to run should their mayor give the word, for by now the ringing was so uneven in tempo and volume, some of them imaged a demented murderer at the bell, luring them to their doom.

But the mayor did not call out. Instead, a loud hoot came from the ringing chamber. The villagers ran to the door and, in an instant, they dissolved into uproarious laughter. The mysterious ringer – the brave citizen, the ghost, the drunkard, the murderer – was none other than a cow nibbling on the straw bell rope hanging down. "The good Lord be praised," said another old woman, "if it isn't old Bessie. Why, she must have headed to the hill for safety."

THE BELL OF
JUSTICE RINGS

In sunny southern Italy, there was an old village, built into a steep hillside. The people in the village were also of a sunny disposition and their king was kind and wise. The king, who lived in the castle above the village, often walked down through the streets greeting his subjects and asking them if they had any problems or needs. He loved his people dearly and wished to make the village a happy and peaceful place.

One day, the king called a village gathering to make a royal announcement. When all were assembled in the square, he spoke: "I wish you to know, my dear subjects, that I am always here to listen to your every need." He pointed to the tower. "There is my gift to you all."

They looked and saw a golden bell, high up on the tower wall. From it dangled a long rope that touched the ground.

"This is the Bell of Justice. Should any of you, rich or poor, be wronged in any way, walk up to the bell and ring for assistance. At the first ring, my counselors will come down to meet you and see that justice is carried out." The king walked over to the bell, holding the long rope in his hands. "And mind you not that you be old or young. As you can see, even the smallest of my subjects can reach this rope."

Over the years of the king's rule, the bell was rung to settle disputes, brawls, and all manner of wrongdoing. Always, as promised, the king's counselors came down to weigh the issues and pronounce judgment. The Bell of Justice became an institution in the village and long after the king died, the bell was still rung.

One day, the head counselor looked at the rope and sighed, "I fear we are not serving the entire village as the king promised. Look at the rope." Indeed the rope was not only badly frayed, but it had also completely rotted away at the bottom. The counselors conferred with one another, then announced: "Since the youngest among you will be unable to ring this bell with the rope's end missing, we shall order a replacement rope be brought to the tower."

But not one rope in the village was long enough to hang to the ground. The counselors sent two young men to a neighboring town to find the replacement rope, then asked the villagers to search about their properties for something suitable in the meantime. Half an hour later, when the crowd assembled again, one villager held up a grapevine covered with leaves. It was long and tough. "Yes," said the counselor fingering the vine, "this will do nicely for now." Another villager climbed up the tower and fastened the grapevine to the bell. All clapped, for the bell could once again be rung by the tiniest of tots.

Now, on the outskirts of the village, there lived a miserly old hermit. He had once been a courageous general, decorated with many war medals – one for every battle in which he had fought. After the war, he settled on his father's farm. With him, he brought his horse, Valor. The horse was so named because the noble beast had carried his master bravely through all the battles.

But as the general grew older, he became bitter. No one cared to hear his war stories. Disillusioned with his neighbors, the general decided to move away from them all. He sold the farmhouse and the many acres of land. He even tried to sell the faithful Valor, but no one was interested in an old horse whose best days were spent. In disgust, the general moved to a forest hut with nothing but a few possessions and some bags of gold.

As for Valor, the general cared not. The old horse was given a swift boot and told to get out. The poor creature hobbled down a country lane, hoping to find a field he might call home. Instead, he was greeted by bully boys, who threw sticks and pebbles at him. On he trod. Dogs growled and barked at him from the verandas of farmhouses he passed by. With nowhere to go, and feeling tired and hungry, the honorable old beast kept following the lane until it turned to cobblestone and led him straight into the village square.

Valor immediately spotted food alongside the tower. He bit down on a grapevine and gave it a tug to break off a chewable size piece. An almighty clang sounded above him and the square soon filled with villagers. The counselors came running to find out what prompted this urgent ring.

"I know that old horse," one villager spoke up, "it's Valor, the poor thing."

Another villager piped up, "Poor thing is right. Why, it's a crying shame the way his master abused him. And to think it was Valor that saved his master's hide more than a couple of times."

One story of Valor's mistreatment followed another and soon the head counselor held his hand up for silence. "The Bell of Justice has been justly rung today. I will send the royal guard to fetch the miserly general. He must atone for his crimes against this poor beast. Valor, you shall have justice."

When the miser was dragged into the village square, the counselor spoke again: "Your noble horse has been faithful and true in service to you for many a year. And how did you repay him? With abuse and abandonment."

The three counselors then turned their backs to the miser and spoke together in low tones. When they turned around, the head counselor looked directly at the old man and said: "We have decided on your punishment – one most fitting for a miser. Half of the gold you carry around in those bags must be given to the court. With that money, Valor will be cared for in grand style. He shall have his very own pasture to graze in at leisure. He shall have a stable fit for a royal steed."

The royal stable keeper led Valor up the hillside to a luscious pasture and a stable behind the castle. "The Bell of Justice has been answered yet again," a villager cheered, and the crowd applauded the brave old horse.

WINTER BELLS

A song and poem about sleigh bells

Merry bells go ring-a-jingle
Nose and fingers freeze and tingle
One and all we sing and mingle
While the snow does fall.

Through the woods and by the river
Hear the cold wind sigh and shiver
And the bells are ringing louder
As we go along.

     – Verse from traditional
     Christmas song

Hear the sledges with the bells,
Silver bells!
What a world of merriment their melody foretells!
How they tinkle, tinkle, tinkle,
In the icy air of night!
While the stars that oversprinkle
All the heavens, seem to twinkle
With a crystalline delight.

> – From "The Bells"
> by Edgar Allan Poe

BELLS IN NATURE
LORE

Sonorous are the bells and drums,
Brightly sound the ringing-stones and flutes.
They bring down with them blessings –
Rich, rich the growth of grain.
They bring down with them blessings –
Abundance, the abundance.

    – Anonymous, 7th century

- In not-so-distant times in Europe, people thought that ringing a bell in a coastal town would bring favorable winds. A bell might even be inscribed with a prayer for fair winds and good weather.
- In Medieval Europe, people believed their church bells would make a pilgrimage to Rome for confession on Good Friday. Should a bell miss the pilgrimage, a poor harvest

or other village woes would result. Bells that made the journey would be returned by the angels in time for ringing in Easter Sunday morning. Children believed the bells carried back Easter eggs for them.

- Long ago in Siberia, people hung bells on sacred trees as an offering carried on the wind.

- In times of draught in ancient China, the emperor sounded the bells with a large wooden ram. Then he knelt to send his prayers for relief up to the heavens with the peal of the bells. The emperor was required to stay kneeling until the rains started. It was believed his power combined with the bells' vibrations to bring showers.

- In Japan, pilgrims readying to climb to the summit of Fujiyama rang a bell and chanted the prayer: "May our six senses be pure and the weather on the mountain be fair."

- Tibetans string spirit bells along with prayer flags on the rooftops of temples as a call for protection. The prayer words are sent on the air as the flags flap in the wind and the bells sound out for all divine powers to heed the requests.

MUSIC OF
THE SPHERES

*Buddhist monks believed their sacred bells allowed the
music of the spheres to be heard on Earth. When Guatama
the Buddha was near death, he described a glorious vision
of the heavenly city of Kasavati to his disciple Ananda, who
wrote down the Buddha's words.*

"The Palace of Righteousness, Ananda, was
hung round with two networks of bells. One
network of bells was of gold, and one was of
silver. The golden network had bells of silver
and the silver network had bells of gold.

"And when those networks of bells, Ananda, were
shaken by the wind there arose a sound sweet, and pleasant,
and charming, and intoxicating. Just, Ananda, as when the
seven kinds of instruments yield, when well played upon, to

the skilful man a sound sweet, and pleasant, and charming, and intoxicating – just even so, Ananda, when those networks of bells were shaken by the wind there arose a sound sweet, and pleasant, and charming, and intoxicating."

> *Bells as musical*
> *As those that, on the golden-shafted trees*
> *Of Eden, shake in the Eternal breeze.*
> – Thomas Moore

II

EVIL BEGONE: RINGING AWAY DARK FORCES

NIGHT OF
THE VAMPIRE

High up in the mountains of China, a small village endured a time of great evil. About three hundred people lived there, but during this excruciating period, the population decreased with the passing of each night. The reason was not epidemic nor earthly catastrophe. The force that fell upon the inhabitants was far worse than anything man might devise. A bloodthirsty vampire scoured the village each and every night, intent on finding his next victim.

The villagers were paralyzed by fear, but they did what little they could to protect themselves. At sunset, every house was bolted closed and the windows boarded shut. The people kept great stones inside their homes and each evening they rolled them in front of their doorways. They cried prayers for protection to the heavens, but every night, just after midnight, a grim figure emerged from his cave, high in the mountains above the village. Silently he descended, his nasty shadow looming menacingly outside the window of his chosen one for the night.

A crash of splintered wood followed by a violent scream made people shudder in their beds, aware the vampire had taken another victim. Day's light revealed the ugly evidence of its visit. Always, the victim lay dead – its eyes open in a look of sheer terror. Its throat bore two savage bite marks and its bedclothes lay about, soaked with blood. Each morning the villagers mourned and buried their dead, then worked until sundown to secure all doors and windows for that night's inevitable attack.

So it had gone on, night after night, for many a week until, in desperation, the villagers sent out a small party to the nearest city, hundreds of miles away, to seek help. By the time the men came back, the village was in a state of panic. The vampire had claimed three weeks' worth of new victims. The villagers ran to meet the returning party, expecting to see bands of men armed and ready to fight off the evil fiend. But there before them was a small old man carrying only a satchel. The villagers began to weep, some shouting words of anger at the party they had trusted to get help.

The leader of the party spoke up quickly: "We have brought you a force far stronger than any sword or club.

This man is a Taoist priest and he is trained in the spirit arts. He has deep and sacred knowledge of how to ward off such evil and end its reign of terror forever."

"There is a way to lure the fiend away from the village and render him powerless," spoke the priest. "I know how to confront evil and triumph." A hushed silence came over the crowd, for they could scarcely believe this wizened old man had such power to command demons. "Although I can confront the vampire, I cannot complete the dark venture without the help of one of you." There were audible gasps and cries, for the villagers had lived in dread for so long, not one of them could imagine confronting the vampire. "I am looking for one who is thoroughly fearless," continued the old priest, "someone who can summon valor from the very depths of his being. This vampire will be most treacherous."

A young man emerged from the group of villagers. "I am that person," he spoke up, "for I detest that fiend from hell. He killed both my brother and sister. I lay in bed and listened to their pitiful screams and knew there was not a thing I could do to help. I have the courage to avenge their deaths."

"Come hither, dear boy," said the priest, "and I shall give you the mighty instruments to fight the fiend." The priest reached into his satchel and presented the boy with two small handbells. "Only do not look so surprised, for these bells are mighty indeed. The sound of ringing metal renders dark forces powerless. Believe me when I tell you, the sound will protect you. But there is one thing you should also be aware of before we set out." The priest spoke solemnly: "Remember, whatever happens, whatever tricks this fiend might try, you must never stop ringing the bells. They must ring without ceasing from sunset to dawn. One moment of silence will strengthen the vampire's powers and you will be doomed." Looking the boy straight in the eye, the priest went on, "Now, young man, do you still have the courage to carry out this nasty task?"

The boy lost no time in his reply: "Yes, dear holy one, I do. I shall never lose faith and together we shall triumph."

The priest then turned to the villagers and said, "I will need you to come with us to the mountain, too."

They all looked fearful and began to step back. But the boy spoke out: "This is truly our only hope. If I can be brave enough to ring the bells, surely you can listen now and follow with faith. It is our last chance and we must take it together."

The priest consulted his holy books and divined that very evening to be a most auspicious time for confronting the vampire. Accordingly, they all set out toward the fiend's mountainous lair, planning to wait there until the sun had set.

When they reached the mountaintop, the priest unpacked his satchel: a holy book, two candles, two bowls, salt, incense, and a gong. All this he placed with great care on a rectangular piece of orange cloth he spread out on the ground. Then he filled the bowls – one with salt and the other with water – and placed them at either end of the cloth. He lit the incense and candles and began to chant.

Soon he motioned to the villagers to form a circle about him. They held hands and they, too, began to chant. As the sun sank below the distant western mountains, a great rumbling came from inside a nearby cave. The villagers tightened their grasp on each other's hands and chanted louder. There was a ferocious growl from behind them, and a sickening stench filled the air. From the dark recesses of the cave appeared a sight so grisly and horrid, many feared they would collapse. But the priest chanted loudly and steadily, and the others knew they must follow or perish.

When the vampire came out to inspect the proceedings, the boy crept behind it and stood at the mouth of the cave. As it moved toward the frightened crowd, it was stopped in its tracks by the ringing of the bells. It swiveled its ugly head toward its cave and let out a vicious snarl. There, blocking the entrance, was the boy, boldly ringing the bells.

The vampire lunged. It howled madly and darted back and forth, trying to unnerve the boy. He did not budge, but rang with even greater resolve. The vampire now moved closer, and the boy thought he might pass out from the smell of the vampire's decaying flesh. Still he rang both bells and still the fiend moved closer. The vampire now came face-to-face with his opponent and glared at him. The boy continued ringing and the two stayed locked in that wretched stare all night long.

As dawn neared, the vampire became frantic at not being able to go back into its cave. It moved forward deliberately and stared deeply into the boy's eyes, as if to hypnotize him. "It is trying to trick you. Ring even louder," yelled the priest, and the momentary sense of enchantment was broken. The boy stared down the fiend and, with his last bit of strength, he rang harder than he had ever rung those bells on that long night.

As the darkness began to lift, the vampire scowled, then roared until the ground about the cave shook. Still the boy kept ringing until at last the sun rose over the far eastern horizon. At that very moment, the vampire groaned and fell to the ground dead.

The villagers let go of their neighbors' hands and the circle disbanded. They quickly gathered tree branches and pieces of wood on the ground about, and lit a huge bonfire. They picked up the body of the vampire and threw it upon the flames. The villagers cheered wildly and hugged one another, laughing and weeping in relief.

No one seemed to notice the boy at the cave entrance. He stood in a trance, still ringing the bells. The priest came over to him, putting an arm about his shoulders. "Dear boy," the priest whispered in his ear, "you have done your job successfully and with immense courage. You have defeated the great evil force. Now you may stop the ringing." The trance lifted from the boy's eyes and, although he appeared alert to the priest's words, still he rang the bells. The priest clutched the boy's hands and gently pried opened his fingers until the bells fell to the ground.

That was many years ago and most of the villagers are dead and gone. But high in the mountains there lives an old man. He is a wise and holy man, and many who search for him recognize him immediately. He sits serenely in his chamber, but his wrists move continuously, as if he were ringing two invisible bells. And he will tell anyone who consults him that his hands have shaken and trembled since that horrible night when he stared evil straight in the face and triumphed. "It was a small price to pay for my village," he humbly replies, and then shares his hard-earned words of wisdom.

DRIVING AWAY
TEMPEST

It is said that evil spirytes that ben in the regyon of th' ayre doute moche when they here the belles rongen when it thondreth, and grete tempeste and outrages of wether happen, to the ende that the feindes and wycked spirytes should be abashed and flee, and cease the movynge of tempest and this is the cause why the belles ben rongen.

— From *Legenda Aurea*
by Wynken de Worde

Tempestuous Bell Lore

In Medieval Europe, evil spirits in the air were thought to be the true cause of wild tempests and thunderstorms. "Metal can break magic and loud noise drives away demons" was a superstitious saying of the times. Bells, being both metallic and loud, were naturally considered an extremely powerful force in the fight against evil. Because they were high up in the belfry of a holy place, people believed bells had direct access to the wicked fiends and spirits thought to be hovering over every village. This was not only the belief of simple village folk, it was also the theory of learned church scholars.

St. Thomas Aquinas is thought to have written this account of the power of bell ringing against evil forces: "The atmosphere is a battlefield between angels and devils . . . The aspiring steeples around which cluster the low dwellings of men are to be likened, when the bells in them are ringing, to the hen spreading its protective wings over its chickens; for the tones of the consecrated metal repel the demons and arrest storms and lightning."

Villagers wanted their houses built near the church to be enveloped by this protective sound. With all those demons battling overhead, it was reassuring to know that the simple clanging of their church bell could instill some terror in the dark forces and that once the evil spirits were gone, the tempests they brought with them would disperse.

At the first sign of a storm cloud or the sounding of a low rumble in the distance, the church sexton or the assigned bellringer would make a dash for the church, rush up the belfry stairs, and ring for all his worth. In belfries, rhymes were posted to strengthen the resolve of these ringers during storms. One in a belfry in Cornwall, England read:

By which are scar'd the fiends of hell,
And all by virtue of a Bell.

There are several thunder bell stories from the south of
Germany near the Alps. Many of the parish churches there
assigned special bells for ringing throughout spells of heavy
weather. Parents even gave their children blessed handbells,
with saints engraved on the metal, to ring outdoors during
storms to protect them from being hit by lightning.

In one town on a lake, bells all over the community were
rung as townsfolk believed the bells' sound would keep them
safe, especially from the power of the lightning bolt. This pas-
sionate belief caused tragedy one time when the townsfolk
rushed to the church belfry to help the bellringer do his job.

They pulled down hard on the bell ropes in hopes of making a greater sound. But the pull caused the bells to swing up higher than usual. Lightning struck the upward mouth of a bell, which, in a flash, conducted through the rope and killed several of the ringers on the receiving end of the electric shock. They were knocked dead to the belfry floor.

Toward the late 1400s, many townsfolk recited prayers as they rang, hoping to gain even greater protection from spirits of the air. They wished to dispel all evil activity in the atmosphere before it could come down to Earth and develop into disease and plagues. The fact was, many believed, that they could never eliminate wicked spirits, but they could hold the demons at bay. When the townsfolk heard the rumble of an approaching storm, they assumed it to be a returning demon. Ringers ran again for their bells.

A tourist traveling through the Tyrolese Alps witnessed bells being rung during storms. His account of that strange event was published in the November 1867 issue of *Blackwood's Magazine*. Here are some of the tourist's impressions:

> The bell-ringing, as the companion of the thunderstorm, is a permanent institution here. Opposite to Tembach, on a spur of the mountain rising right over the river Inn, there is a sort of hermitage or chapel. It is the duty of a recluse who has charge of

it to be on the look-out for thunderstorms, and begin the bellringing; and he is well posted for the accomplishment of his duties. A solemn, strange duty it must be to act as a sentinel against the approach of such a foe.

I happened once to witness the ceremonial ringing out the thunder in a very picturesque shape. I was coming out of the great gorge behind the Martinswand. The first thing that drew attention was a rushing, mighty wind, which caught up the marble powder lying on the hill side, and drifted it about like a dry, sandy mist. Then came, as sudden, a lull and the church bell of Ziri, right under my feet, began "tolling slow, with sullen roar." The chime was taken up by a dozen or so other churches in the valley. Mellowed in the distance till it "passed in music out of sight."

NAMING AND BLESSING
THE BELLS

My name is Susanna, I drive the devils hence.
— Bell inscription in Erfurt, Germany

An eighteenth-century traveler recorded the proceedings of a bell blessing ceremony. He noted that bells were named, baptized, and blessed to make them truly effective fighters of all the demons, fiends, and wicked spirits thought be hovering about in the air. Churches held a christening service for each bell, similar to that of an infant's baptism. The bell was outfitted in a fine cloth garment and given a name. The priest sprinkled water on the bell from the baptismal font, then prayed and blessed the bell to enhance its thunder-fighting power. Wealthy members of the congregation bestowed gifts on their new bell, which the priest received on its behalf.

These consecrated bells were considered the *Vox Domini* – the voice of the Lord – and now held the divine power to stop tempests and drive away all evil forces affecting the air.

Words and symbols were also inscribed on the bell to augment its divine power. When the bell was rung, people believed the air demons would not only hear the sacred sound, but also see the bell's words of intention. When the bell was not ringing, they hoped the symbols would keep the bell safe from attack in the belfry. A cross was often the chosen bell symbol. It was not only a holy sign, but it also looked like the mighty hammer of Thor, the Norse god of thunder.

The bell inscriptions were meant to be read as messages and were often written in the holy language of the Church – Latin. It did not matter that many people in the villages below did not understand Latin, it only mattered that the inscriptions had meaning to the evil forces and, of course, to the helpful angels also hovering above who could bring aid to the battle for earthly souls.

TEMPEST BELL
INSCRIPTIONS

Lightning and thunder I break asunder.
– From a 17th century monastery bell

Dissipo Ventos – I disperse the winds.
Nimbum Fugo – I put the cloud to flight.
Fulmina Frango – I break the lightning.
Fulgura Frango – I break the thunder.
Fulgura Compello – I drive away the thunder.
Defunctos Ploro Caelum Reddonque Serenum – I bewail the
dead, and restore a serene sky.

HELL'S BELLS

The bellman ran through the streets trying to awaken any sleepers with the ringing of handbells. "Fire, fire at the church!" he shouted. Just after midnight, the tower became completely engulfed in flames. Then in one grand shuddering, it collapsed to the ground.

As the hours passed and the fire died down, many of the villagers went back to their homes, lamenting the loss of their beautiful old church, where they had worshipped for years. Only the churchwarden and the village parson stayed behind to examine the ruins. By early morning light, they noticed that although the church steeple and belfry were completely destroyed, to their amazement the bells were untouched by the fire.

Both men were greedy and a fight broke out as each laid claim to the bells. They quarreled loudly until the earth rumbled and shook beneath their feet. Then darkness and an ominous silence hung about.

Suddenly a wild rush of air and a shadowy cloaked figure from the depths of hell swooped down and grabbed the church bells. "The devil himself has stolen our bells!" screamed the churchwarden, paralyzed by the menacing sight. The parson, furious that anyone, even the devil, would dare to take his prize from him, raced to the street to hunt down the demon. He screamed out at the fiend, "Give me back those bells! They're mine."

The parson's rage filled him with the strength of ten men, whereupon he grabbed the demon and spun it about. "I demand you give me the bells back," he yelled.

The devil spun himself faster, screaming and cursing as he whirled: "You are a fool, holy man. How dare you challenge me? I should never surrender these bells, especially to so puny and unworthy an opponent as you, little parson." At this, the devil roared.

Immediately the air became eerily quiet, but a moment later, furious gales blew. Still the devil cackled and screamed: "I shall take these bells with me, straight to hell!" He then leapt up into the air with the peal of church bells. Hovering for one moment, he made a dive right through the earth.

The parson stared in utter amazement as the devil and the bells disappeared beneath the ground into a great abyss. Water immediately filled up the deep hole and within but a few seconds, the hole had become a small pool. As the parson watched, bubbles formed at the center of the pool's surface.

The pool still stands today and bubbles still float along the top. Ask anyone who lives in those whereabouts and they will probably explain how the bubbles are caused by the devil, as he journeys back to hell with the village's stolen bells. The villagers call this unholy sight Hell's Hole.

THE DEMON-FIGHTING
BELL OF ST. PATRICK

St. Patrick, like all early missionary priests, carried bells called cloggas with him as he walked the roads and pathways of the Irish countryside, from one parish to the next. The cloggas were designed for the Celtic father's traveling ministry. They were light in weight, small, and shaped like a cheese grater, with a handle at the top to hold them when ringing. St. Patrick carried several bells on his journeys, and many healing miracles were attributed to them. One of St. Patrick's bells gained a place in legend for its great battle against the forces of evil. This is the saint's bell named the Broken Bell of St. Brigid.

One day, when St. Patrick was walking alone in holy contemplation on his way to his next parish ministry, he became aware of cold gusts of air about him – first from above, then from over in the bushes, then encircling him. This was indeed strange for it was a perfectly calm summer's day. He stood still. Not a tree branch swayed along the roadside ahead of him; not a blade of grass nor a tall wildflower moved in the fields on either side. But all about him was a terrific whirlwind.

He walked on in holy determination, muttering prayers as he strode. Still the winds whistled, gaining fury and turning icier. From the corner of his eye, St. Patrick thought he saw a shape take form in the air, but when he turned his head there was nothing. From the other side he was aware of a hideous cackling laugh, but when he turned, again there was nothing. He stopped to make sense of the oddness of the moment, shuddering, not from coldness, but from a feeling of pure evil surrounding him.

Dark and ghastly shapes began to materialize in the very air. A throng of wretched fiends swarmed in clusters above him and in every direction from where he stood. Their faces were those of utter hellishness. The ugly lot of devils heckled and jeered at St. Patrick. They spat at him and hissed; they whined in hideous tones, then roared with rage.

"Devils from the north," the goodly saint called out, "I command you to be gone from my path." Still they screamed and pestered him until St. Patrick felt the treachery of their horrid clutches. How could he, one man alone amidst a raging mob of fiends, find the strength to resist their powerful attacks? He was a man of peace and carried no weapon. Then he remembered the bell he had tied at the waist of his robe. He unloosed the knot and held the metal out in front of him, ringing the old bell with all the energy he could muster.

Still the demons raged, diving and gnawing at the poor missionary priest. St. Patrick did not flinch; he rang the bell even louder. But the devilish crew had savage strength, powered by fury. They whipped up a storm about the saint until he was blown almost off his feet. With great resolve, St. Patrick hurled the bell straight into the swarming horde. A great *clang* sounded as the bell flew into the devils. The *clang* grew louder and more insistent, then echoed throughout the air. The frightened demons spun about in a daze of terror. As their strength subsided, winds hushed and the air grew warm. The saint once more was able to bask in the serenity of a summer's morning.

St. Patrick looked in the grass, where he knew his bell must have landed. Sure enough, there it lay in the field, shattered and broken from the fall. The missionary priest picked it up and held it reverently as he prayed. He named the bell the Broken Bell of St. Brigid. So powerful was the effect of the ringing on the evil demons that not one dared to set his ugly countenance on Irish soil for seven years, seven months, and seven days.

WICKED SPIRITS
ALL ABOUT

Est Mea Cunctorum Vox Daemoniorum – My voice is the slayer of demons.

In many cultures, the ringing and wearing of bells were to keep dark powers at bay:

- Many many centuries ago, bells were used in China specifically to scare dragons. They were often ornate, with dragons embellishing the handles.
- Chinese noblemen held up small bells called *tos* and shook them at the sky to drive away eclipses.
- Farmers in China fastened tiny bells to their work carts and wheelbarrows when they went to the fields. As the carts were pushed along, they set the bells ringing, which cleared the path of any lingering, fiendish spirits.

- Chinese cities of long ago rang and tinkled with every passing breeze. Small wind-bells were hung from the eaves of houses and pagodas, and about city gates. Even the trees sounded in the wind, for many bells hung from branches of trees lining city streets. The bells would not only register the movement of demonic spirits, but their ringing would drive them away.

- The Great Bell of Peking was thought to be capable of agitating the weather spirits if struck by people not appointed to sound it. If an unauthorized person were to draw back the beam and strike the bell, the great rain god would respond immediately by sending a flood of rain on the city.

- Travelers in the Orient wore a set of bells at their knees in the belief that the bells would protect them in foreign lands.

- Tibetan men often tied a small bell to the end of a length of cord, which was then wrapped around their money. The bell would ward off evil spirits that may have attached themselves to the cash.

- Terrifying faces of the most ferocious gods and goddesses appeared on some Tibetan bells to further scare the evil entities already agitated by their sound.

- In Bali small bells called *gonseng* were fastened to the feet of birds, so that as they flew into the air, the sound of the bells would startle and scatter the fiendish air spirits.

- Young children in some Central African tribes walked with tiny bells on their feet and toes to protect them from attack by evil spirits.
- When wizards and magicians were engaged in fortune-telling or seances, bells were rung to let the spirits know of their intent to contact the other world for answers.
- A bell was rung after uttering a curse to guarantee the curse would hold.
- High priests in Israel wore bells of gold on their hems, as explained in the Old Testament. They believed the sound provided a protective force from demons wanting to invade the sanctuary.

> . . . upon the hem of it thou shall make pomegranates . . . round about the hem whereof; and bells of gold between them round about: A golden bell and a pomegranate, a golden bell and a pomegranate, upon the hem of the robe round about.
> – From Ex. 28. 33–34
> King James Version

ROUTING OUT
WITCHES

Church bells were rung on days when witches and warlocks were known to gather. Villagers expected wicked pranks on the dreaded days of Midsummer's Eve and Walpurgis Night, the eve of May Day. Some medieval villages feared Friday nights, especially those that fell in the month of March. On these dark eves, as well as on Twelfth Night and the fifth night of February – St. Agatha's Eve – it was thought witches could make themselves invisible and haunt the very air of a town.

The only way to fight them during these witching hours was with sound and fire. Church bells rang out from the onset of darkness to the first ray of morning. Below on the streets, a wild spectacle unfolded. Townsfolk paraded through their village shouting and banging pots and pans. Some cracked whips, while others shook small handbells. Dogs were let loose to run and bark throughout the village. Folk carried fiery torches through the streets, chanting and screaming: "Witch flee, flee from here, or it will go ill with thee."

The sole mission of the villagers was to rout out the lot of witches and warlocks living within their gates, especially on the most formidable of witching nights. But the power of witchcraft was feared to be ever present.

There was some comfort in the knowledge, however, that as the townsfolk slept, their streets were being patrolled by the village watchman. While his main job was to maintain lawfulness, he had the additional responsibility of holding the powers of darkness at bay. The watchman carried a handbell and rang it up and down every street and in front of each house. As he rang, he uttered prayers for divine protection and blessings for the people sleeping within. To many in the village, he was simply known as the bellman whom they trusted to keep them safe from harm.

THE BELLMAN

From noise of scare-fires rest ye free,
From murders Benedicte:
From all mischances that may fright
Your pleasing slumbers in the night:
Mercie secure ye all, and keep
The goblin from ye, while ye sleep.
Past one o'clock, and almost two,
My master all 'Good day to you.'
     – Robert Herrick, 1823

RINGING AWAY THE
BLACK DEATH

Pestem Fugo – I drive away pestilence.
   – Northamptonshire bell inscription

The terrified people of fourteenth-century Europe believed the Black Death came from evil spirits lurking everywhere throughout their cities and villages. They rang bells with great fervor, in hopes of driving away these demons of plague and pestilence.

In truth, the bubonic plague arrived in Europe, carried by flea-infested rats. One of the plague's hideous symptoms was that the skin of those suffering turned black. So dreadful and agonizing were the deaths that the plague was labeled the Black Death. It was also called the Great Dying. For more than a hundred years it swept mercilessly across Europe, claiming the lives of almost one-third of the population.

But the people continued to blame evil spirits for the plague. Because the spirits could strike anywhere at any hour, the bells had to be constantly rung, as they would be in a storm. Whole villages were held in the tight clutches of these plague spirits and often the bellringers continued their duty despite their illness. The only sound in these stricken villages was ringing and when it stopped, villagers assumed the plague had claimed another, this time the ringer at the ropes. Quickly another person would rush up the belfry steps to continue the ringing, lest the plague spirits gain ground.

An eerie silence hanging in the air meant most of the villagers were dead, or too sickly to ring. Those still well enough to move about cared for the dying, or collected the dead. And again, a bell marked the horrible occasion. As the carts for bodies made their daily rounds, a bell was rung and the bellman yelled out the gruesome command: "Bring out your dead!"

ILLNESS BELL
LORE

*Let the bells in cities be rung often, and the great ordnance
discharged; thereby the aire is purified.*
>   – Certain Rules, Direction or
>   Advertisements for the
>   Time of Pestillential Contagion, 1625
>   by Dr. Francis Hering

- In the ancient kingdom of Annam in Southeast Asia were
  exorcists whose job it was to ward off the demons of
  illness. Upon entering an infected house, the exorcist
  would begin to jingle the string of bells he had fastened
  on his big toe and strum his lute. He would circle the
  sickbed and walk through the house, shaking his toe bells
  and strumming until he believed the demons had not
  only departed, but were banned.

- In ancient Japan, one of the ways to end an epidemic was to collect the pillows from under the heads of sick people. The pillows were thought to be full of demons and spirits that had brought the epidemic. A long procession of townspeople carried the pillows out of the village to a remote location. The strange parade wound its way through the streets and country roads, accompanied by bell ringing.

- Shamans in central and northern Asia used bells in their healing rituals. They shook and rang bells of all sizes to drive infecting spirits away. Then they purified the area around the sick person with the sound of their bells. They were especially adept at driving out the wicked spirits they believed inhabited the minds of mentally ill persons.

- In China, the shaman rang his handbell not only indoors, but also out-of-doors when called upon to break a drought or drive away cholera demons. Each time after ringing it, he kowtowed to the illness spirit.

III

THE SAGACITY OF BELLS: MIRACLES AND WONDER

THE PIRATE
PUNISHERS

*Long ago, in the north of Britain, warring clans fought con-
stantly with one another. In the midst of all this battling
came peaceful men from across the sea. They were holy men
called monks, who had no desire to choose sides in the
struggle. They kept to themselves and lived a humble exis-
tence, dwelling in caves in the Scottish glens.*

The monks' kindness was felt by even the most
savage of clans. Many clansmen were moved
by their unexpected gentleness. Some, tired of
fighting, joined the monks. Over time, the monks
built an abbey in the glen and the people gave them a peal of
silver bells for the abbey chapel.

While some of the savagery had calmed down in the
land, nasty scoundrels still sailed the Scottish coast. Villages

along the shore lived in constant threat of pillage and plunder by bands of roving pirates. The monks were warned that the pirates held nothing as holy and would find the abbey only too splendid a source of treasure. For over the few years of its establishment, the abbey had been bestowed with gifts of silver and gold, paintings, and valuable objects for worship.

Still, the pirates did not discover the wealthy abbey, for its stone walls appeared to be craggy cairns when viewed from a distance offshore. Whenever pirate activity was reported in the area, the abbot issued a stern warning to the monks: "There is to be no bell ringing until the coast is clear of pirates. Even one ring would alert that wicked band to our precious abbey."

There was a young monk who had just joined the abbey, whose heart filled with joy at the sound of the bells. He thought there could be no other earthly voice so close to the holiness of God. He had delighted in their sound for only a week when news of pirates reached the abbey. The abbot made his announcement: "Rogues have been spotted not far from our shore. By all accounts they mean to rest here long enough to make repairs and put in supplies. Until they are well on their way to other shores, the bells must not be rung."

The older monks quietly went back to their work, but the new monk stared up at the bell tower. "How long must it sit silent?" he worried. At times, throughout those first days, the young monk walked to the chapel and went up to the ringing room, just to touch the ropes and look at the bells. He left quickly, before the temptation to pull on the rope became too strong.

The pirates showed no great hurry to leave the cove. At night their drunken shouts resounded through the glen. Each evening the monks prayed for safety, but the young monk was agitated. He yearned to hear the blessed bells ring. "Just once," he thought, "surely the pirates will be too drunk to even notice." He left his brothers to their prayers and by the evening's fading light, he made his way up the chapel stairs to the ringing room.

"I'll just ring the smallest bell," he thought, "and not so very hard at that." And he pulled that bell's rope very cautiously. Above him came the beautiful note, silvery and strong in the clear evening. The monk listened and when the tone stopped its resounding, he was horribly aware of another silence. No longer was there drunken cussing from the cove. "Perhaps," he reasoned, "it means that the bell's holy sound has driven the rogues away once and for all."

When the young monk came from the chapel, the reality of his action began to set in. "Have you lost your senses, lad?" demanded the abbot in an icy tone. "Surely you know what this silence means."

The monks went to their sleeping quarters that night and waited, wide-awake in the terrifying silence.

At the first clatter at the gate, the monks ran to the chapel to await the abbot's instructions. "Bar the main doors," he commanded. When they had done so, the abbot turned to them with a calm expression on his face. "No panic now, but we must be quick. We will all leave by way of the east gate. You will leave in partners and each pair will fill a chest with valuables and carry it between you."

"But where are we going?" asked the young monk.

"Just follow your brothers," the abbot said calmly. "We will hide out at our first home in the caves. God be with you all."

Quickly, but with the utmost order, each chest was piled with candlesticks, goblets, paintings, and church relics. The monks retreated quietly through the chapel's east exit, heading straight for their caves in the hills.

The abbot was the last to leave and as he made his way out, he heard the main door of the chapel come crashing down. The drunken band of pirates entered the holy room with roars of laughter. Seconds later, they were shouting and cursing when they realized there was no treasure to raid. "The bells," yelled their wicked captain, "at least there's something of value left. We'll melt them down for ship cannons and ammunition."

The abbot heard these shocking words from his place in the shadows and listened in agony at the pirates racing up the belfry stairs. The old abbot held the cross he had saved from the chapel high in the air and called on God to show his almighty wrath at this unholy insult. Then he closed the side door and ran into the night to safety in the caves.

The dreadful noise from high in the belfry carried through the night air. The pirates swore while the bells clanged. Finally the bells were pulled from their ropes and dragged down from the chapel to the shore. The stolen bells were then crammed into the hold of the pirate ship.

The captain and two of the pirates stayed behind at the abbey, with evil determination in their hearts. "We'll show you, monks, what happens to those who dare to double-cross pirates," the captain yelled into the night. He grabbed a torch from the chapel wall and tossed it at the huge tapestry hanging above the altar. Within seconds, the old abbey was up in flames and the pirates ran back to the shore.

As their ship set sail, the captain and his men roared with vicious laughter at the sight of fire in the glen. So loud was the merriment aboard that at first they did not hear the sound coming from below deck – from down in the hold. The small bell began to ring, quietly at first, but steadily. As its tone swelled, the second bell of the peal began to ring out, then the third, the fourth, and then the last and heaviest tenor bell, with its low loud toll. At this final bell, the crew became silent. All listened as the peal in the hold grew louder and stronger.

"The bells are sounding the death knell," cried out one of the pirates, and immediately the crew was seized with panic. At this moment, the seas picked up and the winds grew to gale force. But all about, the sails hung slack and the ship rocked violently in the massive waves.

"Curse those bells," the captain shouted as he raced to the hold and opened it wide. The sounds of the bells were deafening now. "Throw them in the sea," he commanded his terrified crew.

As the pirates moved forward to remove the bells, the bells grew louder and the men stood trembling. They watched as the bells in the hold below started to increase in size. With each toll, they grew. The ship began to creak and groan at the weight of the massive bells. With the thudding vibration of the death knell and the immensity of the bells, the ship gave a great shudder and every timber split. As the pirate ship sank and the last screams from the shipwrecked crew faded below the ocean waves, the bells could still be heard tolling from the deep.

Come morning light, the monks who had witnessed the wild event from shore resolved to rebuild their abbey. In time, the new monastery was established and a new peal of five bells was blessed and hung in the tower. The monks remembered their faithful old peal in a prayer, then began to ring the new. After the five bells sounded, an echo reverberated far off in the bay – a muffled and watery ringing that might be coming from the very bottom of the sea.

THREE
MIRACLE BELLS

. . . a bell that was more famous than great, more valuable in reality than appearance, because it exceeded every organ in sweetness of sound: it condemned the perjured; it healed the sick; and what appeared more wonderful, it sounded every hour without anyone moving it . . .

– Account of the Bell of St. Teilo from the
Liber Landavensis, 1133c

In the late fifth to the seventh centuries, missionary monks arrived in Britain to spread their Christian beliefs. These early Celtic fathers walked throughout the countryside well into the farthest reaches of the British Isles. People heard them coming by the sound of the ringing bells they carried in their hands, or wore around their waists on rope belts. They rang these bells throughout Cornwall, Wales, Scotland, and Ireland to gather people to hear their evangelical words.

The Celtic bells were often hardly different in appearance than simple sheep bells. They were not cast, but forged or hammered by metalsmiths, who designed them to be small and lightweight with handles, so they could easily be held. The missionary monks in Ireland called their traveling bells clogga.

While these handheld bells may have been crude in appearance, several were considered as rare and valuable as if they had been cast from pure gold. These Celtic missionary bells were reputed to have performed great miracles on their travels. So valued were these bells that when danger of theft threatened, some were buried in hallowed ground or chained in a sanctuary. Other famous miracle bells were housed in gold and jeweled shrines, built especially for their safekeeping.

The Miracle Bell of St. Mura

Loud ringing came from high in the skies above the small Irish village of Fahan in County Donegal. "A bell from heaven itself," people exclaimed, as they stared straight up on that clear sunny day almost thirteen hundred years ago. The wondrous bell hovered overhead, ringing out it angelic tones. The people below fell to their knees and raised their arms to the heavens. "Glory be," they shouted, and they watched in awe as the bell began to move toward them. Some were frightened by the magnitude of the event, for never before had heaven sent such a miracle. Some feared the splendid sound was really meant as a warning of doom, and they huddled together in fright.

The ringing grew louder as the bell descended, then the bell hovered and released one resounding tone of sheer beauty. The people gasped at the power of that holy sound. But at that moment, the bell began to shake. The bell's clapper seemed to be falling out of the bell and, at the next moment, it became completely detached and began to float in thin air. Then, as the whole village watched, the clapper ascended back up to heaven. Although no words were heard from on high, the people below understood that the bell was too holy to be heard on the earth. They bowed their heads in honor of the greatness of the divine gift. At that prayerful moment, the heavenly bell dropped in the field.

St. Mura picked up the sacred object and held it out to show the people. The bell looked to be made of bronze, with silver and gold plating, and was decorated with elaborate brass knotting and a sparkling circle of gems and amber. In the center, set in gold, was a large crystal. It glowed brilliantly in the saint's hands. All those who witnessed the scene felt renewed of spirit and light of heart.

The bell became known as the Bell of St. Mura and many were the miraculous powers and events attributed to it. One woman said that her husband had been near death with a lingering illness when he was allowed to drink water from the bell. Immediately color returned to his pale face and the strength returned to his legs. He leaped out of bed, dressed in a flash, and danced a jig that same night at a village gathering. The bell, he said, was like an elixir. Another woman, who had not been able to see or hear since a childhood fever, took one sip from the bell and filled her senses with all the beauteous sights and sounds about her.

Word spread of the curative powers of the Bell of St. Mura. It seemed to have a particularly helpful effect on women during childbirth. One drink from the amazing bell and pain was relieved. Babies were born with ease.

St. Mura went on to build his abbey, on the exact spot where the miracle bell had fallen from heaven so many years before.

The Golden Butter Miracle Bell

St. Odoceus was a monk with an air of great mystery about him. As he walked throughout the Welsh countryside in the valley of Llandaff, people watched and whispered: "He walks as one not quite of this earth."

On one especially hot afternoon, St. Odoceus of Llandaff stopped at a fountain in the vale for a drink of water. There he saw two young women washing their butter, for that was the customary way to prepare it. "Pray, might I have a vessel from which to drink?" he asked. The two girls giggled and, holding up the butter in their hands, they answered: "This butter is all we have for a cup. Do you think you might drink from it?"

St. Odoceus took the cold and wet butter, molding it until it looked like a small bell. He then held it under the fountain and offered them a drink from the bell cup. They were shocked and refused, so the monk drank his fill. Then he thanked the girls and said: "My thirst is indeed quenched. Bless you for your kind help and generosity on such a hot day." At this, St. Odoceus lifted the butter up to the sun, then held it out to them in the cradle of his hands. "Here, then, is your butter," he said, and one of the girls reached out and took it.

The young women watched as he walked away, then one gasped: "Quick, remember the butter in your hands. It will surely melt in this hot sun." The girl holding the butter went to put it under the cold water when she, too, gasped: "Only look. It remains in the form of the bell." Her friend tapped at the brilliant golden object she held in her hands. "This is hard as metal," she said, breathless. "In fact, it seems to be made of gold." Indeed it was pure gold.

Just then an old man, who had been ill for many months, approached the fountain. He was bent over and coughing loudly. "What is that golden bell in your hand, young miss? Why, it is the color of butter." When he reached out to touch it, something wondrous happened. The old man, who had arrived hunched over in pain, stood straight for the first time in years. He then breathed a strong healing breath deep into his lungs.

The girls were startled at the immediate visible change. The sick old man appeared to be in perfect health and at least twenty years younger than he had been before touching the bell. "This golden bell is unlike any other. It is indeed a holy bell," the girls cried out.

They picked up the bell and took it straight to the church in Llandaff. There it was hung up and dedicated to holy work. And from that day forward, great numbers of people have come to see and touch the bell. Many testified that the Bell of St. Odoceus was indeed a true miracle bell, for one touch was said to restore health to the ill and vitality to the tired.

A Bell to Cure Madness

St. Fillan traveled throughout Scotland with a bell that was bigger than most carried by other missionaries. His bell stood higher and had the appearance of a tall metal hat. Perhaps that is how the idea to put it on people's heads first came to St. Fillan. He would place the bell on a sick person's head and immediately they felt at ease.

St. Fillan's Bell brought the greatest relief to the mentally ill. Word of the miraculous bell cap spread, and folk traveled great distances to meet up with the saint, bringing an afflicted person along with them. Sometimes it was an old uncle or a sister who the doctor had diagnosed as stark raving mad and the village had labeled a lunatic. St. Fillan merely put the bell over the afflicted one's head, and the veil of insanity that had clouded their eyes for years suddenly lifted. The families thanked St. Fillan, for now they could go about their lives without deep shame and the need to keep family secrets.

Stories of the bell's miracles were many by the time the saint died. A chapel was built and named for St. Fillan's Bell. But people remembered the saint's healings and some wondered if the bell would not still possess the healing touch on its own.

Great ritual was adopted over the years. To cure the insane, the bell from the chapel was placed on a tombstone in the old churchyard. Then, that very night, an insane person was brought to the chapel, where he was dipped, sometimes screaming and cursing, into the saint's pool. He was sent home with instructions to be brought back the following day. The bell was returned to the chapel, where it was bound securely with ropes for the night. The next evening, bell and "lunatic" were taken together into the graveyard. There, the bell was ceremoniously placed upon the head of the mad person, who was then tied down and left alone all night with the bell on his head. The next morning, when the priest returned, the bell was solemnly removed. The person, it was believed, would be mad no more.

INDIGNANT BELLS

Many a bell has been known to have a strong "mind" of its own. Some monks chronicled accounts about bells that refused to ring anywhere but their home bell tower. One such event happened in France in 615 A.D. Bells have a long memory and can carry a fondness for their old church forever.

The king of France was visiting Burgundy when he heard the most spectacular ringing coming from the church tower in Sens. The sound filled him with great joy and passion. As he was readying to leave for Paris, the king was haunted by the splendor of the church bell. "I must have that bell taken to Paris, for its sweet tones can touch so many more people," he explained.

And so the bell was carefully taken from the tower of St. Stephen's and loaded onto a cart by the royal guards. The bishop of Sens was most upset. He made gentle protests to the king, telling him how important the bell was to the hearts of every citizen of Sens. The bishop then wept; he truly could not imagine his beautiful church without its sweet ringing. But the king was unmoved. The powerful feelings inspired by the bell had captured his own heart, and his thoughts were only of the glorious new addition to Paris.

On the road heading home, the king stopped his royal party to inspect the bell, to ensure it was safely packed and would not be damaged. One of the guard's swords fell hard against the bell during the safety check. The guard was frantic he would be punished, but the bell made no sound. There should have been a great clanging of metal.

The guard knocked on the bell with his helmet. Still no sound. "Your Majesty, come here at once. Something is not right with the Bell of Sens," he cried. King Clotaire II made his way back to investigate. "The bell has gone dumb, sire," explained the guard.

The king tried striking the bell with other pieces of metal and with wood. No sound came forth. Exasperated by the silence, he ordered his guards to hang the bell from a strong tree limb to test it. Perhaps it would sound, away from the muffle of the cart's straw. Once secured, it was struck with great force. Not a tone, sweet or wretched, sounded. King Clotaire II knew the bell would never sound. "Cut down the indignant bell and send it back," he proclaimed.

Another inexplicable marvel was to happen on the road back to Sens. As the king's party made its way toward the city, the bell in the cart began to sound. At first it was just a faint *clang* here and there when the cart hit a pothole, but it soon escalated into full and clear ringing. "I do believe that the bell is rejoicing," said the king's chief minister, who was leading the return.

And so, the Bell of Sens had its way. It was restored immediately to the bell tower of St. Stephen's Church, where it rang forever after with its same sweet and thrilling tone. No one knows exactly what happened that day. Many believed the bell was expressing its sympathy for the bishop; others thought the bell was angry and simply refused to cooperate when taken against its will. Still others felt the bell was sad and lonely away from its home and could not ring for sheer grief. Whatever the reason for its silence on that strange day, all agreed the bell had made an unshakable decision never to cry out anywhere but Sens.

BELLS THAT KNEW
THE TRUTH

Some bells proved to be extremely helpful in matters of the law. St. Selan carried a golden bell with him as he traveled throughout Ireland. Many people would seek him out on his journeys to establish justice in matters that could not be resolved. Men who claimed they had been falsely accused of crimes escaped from jail and ran to find St. Selan to right their wrong.

The old missionary simply gathered witnesses, then asked each person involved in a particular dispute to step forward and touch the bell. With their hand on the metal, St. Selan had them swear that they spoke the entire truth. He cautioned them that if they were not speaking truthfully, the bell would punish any liar.

After St. Selan died, his famous bell of justice was kept well guarded. From time to time, the bell was used to determine guilt or innocence. The thought of the bell punishing the liars was often powerful enough to cause the guilty parties to refuse to partake in the ritual. Perhaps the true power of St. Selan's Bell lay in the fact that fear of punishment was enough to catch the liar. The person's own belief in the power of the bell was possibly the true miracle of justice.

There was another truth-discerning bell in Scotland. Once again, a person would put his hand on the bell and swear his truth. The Scottish bell would sound loudly at the first utterance of falsehood. At times, this bell was called on in matters of allegiance, when people were asked to swear an oath to the king.

A BELL FOR THE
SWEET OF HEART

Gildas was an abbot in ancient Wales, and many studied with him to gain spiritual knowledge. The old abbot was also famous for his crafting of metal into bells. All his bells were considered miraculous for one reason or another. Stories of his miracle bells have been passed down over many generations.

The abbot Gildas had finished the last bit of metal-work on one of his bells. He blessed it and called in one of the abbey's messengers. "I want you to deliver this bell immediately to Bishop David. Tell him it is a token of our great friendship and that, as I crafted it, I knew the bell would ring only for a holy man, sweet of heart," Gildas instructed.

The messenger started out on the long road that would lead him through deep woods and mountainous regions.

He knew that many who fled persecution from the king would be hiding along the route, and he prayed for safety. Gildas had told him not to worry, for the bell would act as strong protection.

As the messenger monk was walking past a rocky area, he noticed a cave. At that very moment, the bell inside his satchel began to ring sweetly. He was shocked, and took off his bag to open it. He carefully lifted out the bell and watched in amazement as the bell continued to sound, without being shaken, tapped, or moved in any way.

The young monk fell to his knees and prayed, so miraculous was the moment. When he lifted his head, he saw an old man coming from the cave entrance. He was dirty and unkempt. The monk knew he was a mountain hermit, and hoped he was one of the harmless holy men who had fled persecution by taking refuge in the mountains.

"That is a sweet and holy sound," said the hermit in a sweet and holy voice. "You have no need to be frightened; I will not hurt you. My name is Illtyd." The young monk was relieved. The hermit picked up the bell and began to ring it. The sound again was so sweet, the messenger once more fell into prayer.

"Young man," said the hermit, "where are you going with this holy bell?"

The monk answered, "My abbot Gildas sends me to deliver this bell to the bishop David."

The hermit smiled, then walked silently back to his cave. The messenger continued on his way to the bishop's church. There he presented the bell, delivering the message from Gildas.

The bishop laughed when he heard Gildas's message: "So he made the bell for a holy man, sweet of heart." At this, the bishop picked up the bell and shook it. There was no sound. He checked the clapper; it was hanging free. The bishop shook it again, then tapped it. No matter how the bell was struck or shaken, it did not make a sound.

"Was the bell sounded by anyone else along your path? Think you now and speak up," he said.

The messenger told the story of how the bell had sounded on its own as he passed a mountain cave. He described the hermit who emerged and the holy tones the bell had rung.

"Did he tell you his name?" asked the bishop.

"He said his name was Illtyd."

"St. Illtyd," said the bishop with great reverence. "He is a holy man in hiding for these many years. He is kind and, yes, most sweet of heart. He would have treasured that bell, but was much too humble to ask for it."

After trying to ring the bell again, the bishop sighed: "I want you to take this bell to Illtyd of the mountain. Tell him that it was truly made for him."

The messenger did as asked. As he arrived at the cave, the bell once more began to ring out sweetly. A smile crossed the old hermit's weathered face, and tears welled up in his kind eyes.

"Tell Gildas that I will ring his bell for the angels who visit me here, and they will be most pleased." The gentle old man walked back to his cave as the messenger continued on his way. The bell was ringing loudly behind him and all about echoed sweetness, as if the very rocks and hills were ringing.

BENKEI AND
THE BELL

Lantern and bell, which is the heavier?
– Old Japanese saying

Many centuries ago, a most curious-looking figure could be seen roaming the mountains and hillsides of Japan. He was one of the countryside's wandering priests. His name was Benkei and he was indeed a spectacle to behold. Rumors spread that the priest was well over eight feet tall and as strong as ten oxen. Some said he could take on one hundred men in combat and win. The giant priest wore a six-sided monk's cap to cover his shaven head. Each day at noon, he would stop along his travels to rest and eat. More often than not, he would capture his meal by shoving his arm straight into the flow of a waterfall and grabbing a big fish. Then

Benkei would down his lunch with rice wine, which he drank straight out of the conch shell he always carried at his waist.

One day, Benkei stopped to rest along the shores of Lake Biwa. As he gazed out at the clear stretch of blue water, he heard the most glorious sound – a shimmer that echoed over the lake and seemed to resonate in the mountains all around. The bell's tone thrilled Benkei to the very depths of his being. "The Bell of Miidera," he said reverently, for he had heard many stories of this marvelous bell. It was a huge temple bell and when it was struck, it made a sound that brought on profound meditation in even the most unholy of men. Some said it was the work of the Buddha himself. The bell had been stolen many times over the years because of its beautiful tones. Now it finally had a home at the monastery of Miidera.

As Benkei listened, his thoughts darkened: "I must have that bell that I may be able to hear its beauty whenever I wish." Benkei imagined the great bell ringing from the belfry in his home monastery. With the bell there, he could visit it on each return and feed his tired body and spirit. "Yes," he hissed aloud, "I must have that bell and I will take it this very night."

By the light of the full moon, Benkei crept up the worn stairs that led to the bell tower. The monastery was silent, as most of the monks were sound asleep. He kept his thoughts focused on the task: how best to remove the bell. With one swift movement of his giant arm, Benkei unhooked the monastery bell. He could not grasp it well and held tight to the bell's sides to make his escape. At first, he considered simply throwing it down to the steep hill below so that it would roll, but he did not want the noise to betray him. He thought to wear it on his head, but worried it would be difficult to see down the stairs and on the long walk home. All of a sudden, Benkei knew the answer. He sat the bell on one hip while he ripped the crossbeam out from the tower. He then suspended the monastery bell from the beam's end behind his shoulder. He wondered how he would balance the massive weight. Benkei then took a paper lantern hanging overhead and hung it from the front end of the beam. "Which is heavier," he wondered aloud, "lantern or bell?"

Slowly Benkei descended the tower stairs, then went down the hill toward his own monastery seven miles away. When he finally arrived, he yelled at the top of his lungs: "Wake up, the lot of you, for I, Benkei, have brought you a marvel." Candles were lit and the sleepy priests shuffled through the corridors toward Benkei, who stood smiling in the main courtyard. "Up to the belfry immediately," Benkei instructed them, "for this bell must be heard to ever be believed."

Benkei described the holy sounds of the bell and how once they heard it ring, they would be forever transformed. The priests followed behind him up the steep and narrow belfry stairs, all of them in awe of his mighty strength and daring. They removed the old bell and mounted Benkei's bell securely on the belfry platform. The giant priest then pulled back on the ramming beam and aimed for the striking point of the bell. "Listen now to sheer glory," he cried, as he sent the beam forward to strike the bell.

Glory it was not. The bell let out a fearful wail. Then the sound tapered off to a whimpering cry: "I want to go back to Miidera! I want to go back to Miidera!" And then one long, final, and most insistent moan: "I WANT TO GO BACK TO MIIDERA!"

The priests gasped. "What a haughty bell it is you have brought us, Benkei," said one of them. "Yes," agreed another, "it thinks our monastery inferior to its own and now it demands to go back." They all laughed heartily and Benkei trembled with rage at the bell's betrayal.

But the oldest priest shook his head and said, "I believe I know what is causing its wailing. Bring me a bowl of sacred water. Once we sprinkle it with this water, the bell will sing out rejoicings in its new home."

Minutes later, a young priest brought in the bowl of water and it was sprinkled over the bell to consecrate it. "The bell is now dedicated to our use," the old priest uttered solemnly.

Once again, Benkei pulled back on the ramming beam and sent it hurling toward the bell. Again the bell wailed: "I want to go back to Miidera!" This so enraged Benkei that he charged forward and seized the rope. He strained every muscle to pull back the ramming beam, then let fly it with force enough to crack the bell. For a moment, a dense sound filled the ears of all. But as the vibrations died away, the bell whined: "Miidera! I want to go back to Mi-i-de-ra!"

Whether struck at morning, noon, or night, the bell uttered the same words. No matter when, by whom, how hard or how gently it was struck, the bell moaned its lament.

At last Benkei unhooked the bell, shouldered it – beam and all – and set off to take it back. He carried the bell to the top of the mountain and set it down. Then, with a fierce kick, he sent it rolling down the valley toward Miidera. There he let it sit. When the Miidera priests found it, they rolled it home and hung it up again. From that day forward, the Bell of Miidera has sounded like any ordinary bell, although the glory of its wondrous sound lived on in the hearts of the old monks.

Over the years, stories of the great bell have been told, and Benkei's feat, though malicious, has become legendary. Talk turned to proverb, and folk in Japan still may laugh and say to one another: "It's like trying to balance a bronze bell with a paper lantern," when any situation appears to be out of balance.

PUNISHING BELLS

Two tales of thieving bellmakers

There was once a Swiss monk named Tancho, whose bell-making skill was renowned. He produced a bell of such glorious tone that people came from all over Europe just to hear it ring. The emperor Charlemagne, himself, arrived with his entourage to witness the bell's splendor. Upon hearing it, Charlemagne commissioned a bell to be made of as sweet a ringing tone. He gave Tancho two bags filled with silver coins – one as payment to the monastery, the other to add to the bell metal, for Charlemagne had heard that silver sweetened the sound.

Tancho took both bags back to the monastery. He spilled the contents onto the foundry table. He looked at both piles of coins. "My bells sound so sweet as they are,"

Tancho mused aloud, "surely no one would be the wiser if this silver was not added to the furnace." And Tancho began to count the coins. "My great skill is the reason for the bell's tone. Surely I deserve more silver than just the one bag," and he placed his hands on either side of the piles and pushed them together to make one gleaming heap of coins. "Besides, any fool knows, too much silver makes for a piercing ring."

Tancho put the coins back in their bags and hid them in a cupboard high above the table. Then he set about designing the emperor's bell. When he had calculated a substitute mix of inferior bell metals, the monk began the casting. A fortnight later, Tancho supervised the bell's hanging in the monastery belfry. Afterward, as he sat alone in the belfry, he examined his bell. "This bell looks like the other and there is no one skilled enough to detect my deceit," he laughed to himself.

He stood at the mouth of the bell and looked at its gigantic clapper. Holding the bell rope in his hands, he thought to move over on the platform and give the bell a ring to prove once and for all, no one in the monastery or the surrounding town or the emperor himself would be able to hear the difference in tone. But his feet would not move and the rope in his hand began to stir. The clapper swung hard to the left without sounding the bell, then forcibly back toward the right, where Tancho stood. With one movement the clapper hit the monk, knocking his head hard against the side of the bell. The dying monk's head became the clapper that sounded his false bell. All who heard the dull ring knew the truth of the matter.

In another European monastery, an abbot set about to build a great basilica. Since there was no foundry in the monastery, the abbot employed a bellmaker from the town to cast a bell for the basilica's tower. The bellmaker was instructed to spare no expense. "I know nothing of your art," confessed the abbot, "therefore, I trust you will prepare a list of what metals you need to guarantee the bell's splendor."

The bellmaker delighted in the abbot's naiveté. "The stupid old fool," he muttered as he drew up his list of metals. "He'll never know if I use gold or copper." At this he made an elaborate request for bags of gold and silver coins, as well as other metals in quantities much greater than needed for one bell.

The next day, a cart arrived from the monastery filled with materials for the great bell. The bellmaker added but a few of the copper pieces in the cart to a heap of old bells he had broken up for recasting. He hid the rest of the precious metals from the cart under the floorboards of his storage room. Then he went about his job of melting down the copper and old bells.

When the bell was cast and cooled, the bellmaker brought it to the basilica tower. The monks never knew the difference as the bell made quite a lovely tone. Its ringing carried over the whole of the town. But every time the basilica bell sounded, and it was rung hourly throughout the day, it had a peculiar effect on one of the townspeople. For the rest of his life, whenever the bell was rung, the thieving bellmaker fell to the ground at its sound and barked like a dog. The bell saw that justice was served.

IV

BIRTH OF
A BELL:
A MIX
OF METALS

THE SOUL OF THE
GREAT BELL

A golden wave of sound floods the air above Old Peking.
Ko-ai. *The thunderous melody rumbles and sets hundreds
of pagoda bells shaking.* Ko-ai. *Its joyous ringing spreads
for miles across the city, and the people below say: "Listen
to the voice of the Great Bell."* Ko-ai *it sings out,* Ko-ai. *As
the golden waves subside, there is a soft sound, like a silvery
whisper,* hsieh, *and mothers tell their children: "Hush, now.
Hark. Do you hear her? It is Ko-ai crying out for her lost
slipper." And the people stop to listen with reverence. They
remember their bell is unlike any other, for the Great Bell of
Peking is a bell with a soul. And those who have not heard
the story listen to hear how the Great Bell came to have a
soul and a voice to cry out.*

Over five hundred years ago, Yung-Lo was emperor of China. From the window of the Imperial Palace, he looked out over his great city of Peking, reflecting on the many wonders he had brought to his people. He had built a magnificent and stately wall to protect his city and had filled Peking with many beauteous sites. There were golden-roofed temples and pagodas strewn with delicate silver bells that sang in the wind. "Life in my city is good," he mused.

But as Emperor Yung-Lo surveyed the world he created, one splendor was missing – a sound he longed to give his great city. "Peking," he decided, "needs to have a great bell." Most of the people never thought about a city bell, for life within the fortressed walls was orderly. The time of day did not require a great ringing bell, for time was told by fire and water. Yung-Lo sighed, moved away from the window, and summoned his ministers to the council chamber.

"The time has come," he told them. "Peking must have a great bell. A voice of gold and silver, powerful enough to be heard for hundreds of miles around." He spoke excitedly. "Imagine a great bell to warn of danger. With one booming chime, the gates of the city would open or close." Then he ordered his ministers: "Find the perfect bellmaker to create this bell for the city and find him now. He must cast a bell so powerful and pure of tone, all other bells will be diminished in comparison. It must be a grand bell, unlike any the world has ever known before."

The ministers, who had taken in every word of their mighty emperor, looked nervous at such a huge command. "Emperor, such a bell would cost a fortune," they exclaimed.

"Then so be it. We must have a bell as splendid and glorious as Peking. Although the bell will hang from the center of our city, its tones must reach into the far country-side. Yes, we must have this bell now," roared the emperor.

The ministers bowed as Yung-Lo left the council chamber. "Whatever shall we do?" fretted one minister.

"Perhaps this bell is truly impossible to create," bemoaned another.

But the third minister spoke calmly: "There is only one thing to do. We must locate the founder who can make it a possibility." And all agreed that when the emperor expressed a wish, they must be prepared to move heaven and earth to make it so. For it was death to all who failed to deliver.

For days, the ministers interviewed the bell-founders of Peking. Each and every man declared such a bell was beyond their scope. Many were convinced there was no one for the job because the bell was impossible to cast. Nevertheless, all were required to remain at the palace to serve as assistants to whomever was chosen master bell-founder.

When the search was exhausted, the senior minister started from his chair and shouted: "I believe I have solved our dilemma. Why did I not think of this before? Kuan-yu, the imperial cannon molder, is the obvious choice for this assignment. I have heard his cannons are the grandest in all the country." So together the three ministers sat down and composed a royal order detailing the services required of the old cannon maker.

Kuan-yu lived in a small village, just outside the walls of Peking, in a modest house with his wife and daughter, Ko-ai. Ko-ai was sixteen and beautiful in every way. Some said her face was more lovely than a peony; others said she had the gentle grace of a butterfly; even others remarked that for all her physical beauty, her heart was more beautiful still. For indeed, Ko-ai extended a deep and loving kindness to all, especially to her parents.

Ko-ai watched, with an ache in her heart, as her dear father ambled to the door on the day the imperial messenger came to their home. He was handed a message, written on brilliant sun-yellow silk and sealed with the emperor's symbol – a red and golden dragon. Ko-ai and her mother waited for Kuan-Yu to say something. He stood in silence, a look of deep worry sweeping across his usually untroubled face.

"What is it, dear father?" Ko-ai finally asked.

Kuan-Yu let the silk scroll drop down to its full length. He read:

Kuan-Yu, master cannon molder, you are hereby summoned by His August Personage, the emperor Yung-Lo, Son of Heaven, to design and cast a great bell for the city of Peking. The bell shall be of a tone worthy of the city's beauty and might. It must ring as clear and rippling as flowing water and as sweet as the sound of a nightingale. It must also be as strong and powerful as any cannon ever made, for its knell must resound through every hill and valley for one hundred miles.

Furthermore, the great bell is to be inscribed in perfect calligraphy, with the most enlightened words of the sages and the holiest words of the holiest men. The greatest stories of China shall be written on the bell. The bell is to then be decorated with symbols of your emperor's majesty and might. It will be his greatest legacy.

The finest foundry is at your command. Any assistant or material you require shall be supplied. Should you fail in this task, death awaits.

At this the old man's hand trembled and his voice shook. "Oh, whatever am I to do? A cannon and a bell may both be made of brass, but their castings are two most different arts. This bell; it is impossible."

Ko-ai spoke gently but firmly to her father: "You shall make this bell. Do not lose faith. It is a great task, yes – one that will require passion and order. The bell will be perfect, my father. You will see."

"Passion and order," said the old man. "Yes, passion and order." And he sounded more confident each time he repeated his sweet Ko-ai's words.

Early the next morning he walked into the city, arriving just as the little dragon bells were ringing in houses throughout Peking. At the Imperial Palace, he met with his assistants at a foundry bigger than he had ever imagined. He quickly discerned the masters in the assembled crowd and assigned them their tasks. "Find the perfect combination of metals and alloys to meld into the bell," he directed the master alchemist. "Listen to the song of every nightingale in the kingdom to find the most flawless singer," he instructed two bell-founders who had impeccable musical ears. "Design and prepare the perfect molds" was his command to the bellsmiths. He employed the most highly skilled artists to engrave symbols and inscribe intricate calligraphy on the bell molds. The others were left to construct a crucible of the giant proportion needed to heat such a large amount of metal.

Then Kuan-Yu headed straight to the imperial library, where he sought the most profound thoughts of holy men and sages through all of China's history. "Passion and order," he muttered over and over to himself, like a meditation to the gods.

The team of masters worked in shifts over a stretch of many days. Kuan-Yu walked back to his village each night for a few hours of quiet rest with his loving family. He looked older and wearier, his heart heavy with strain. There Ko-ai calmed him with her sweet singing. All night she sang and worked on her embroidery in an effort to stay awake should her father need her. She embroidered nightingales, pine boughs, and chrysanthemums on the golden orange dress she planned to be married in someday. From time to time, she stopped to rest her eyes on her sweet father's face. He appeared so worried, even in sleep. Kuan-Yu always woke with a start and ran out of the house, straight for the gates of the city. And each morning, Ko-ai put down her embroidery and fell to her knees to pray for her troubled father.

New shipments of the finest metals arrived daily from across the country and were piled on the foundry floor, for the alchemists had finally calculated the perfect formula. The Great Bell's voice, they determined, would be made sweetly sonorous with brass, ring still deeper with pure gold, and shimmer with the high-ringing tones of silver. Still no one

could be exactly sure of the results, for never had so great a
bell been cast.

Preparations were soon under way. The clay mold was
set in place, fires lit under the cauldron, and firewood gathered and stacked high to keep the great fire burning. Once
the metals were added in their proper proportions, the
emperor and his ministers were notified that the bell was
about to be cast.

The emperor's whole court was in attendance. Musicians
played a royal fanfare as the emperor made his way to the
end of the platform overlooking the steaming cauldron. He
waved his jeweled fan to signal the proceedings. A resounding gong sounded and the cauldron of molten metal was
tipped and emptied. Glowing liquid rushed toward the clay
mold below. Steam and metallic vapors hissed until the
casting was complete.

Kuan-Yu remained for the five days it took the bell to
cool. Then, the clay mold was removed. The founders hung
their heads in shame and despair. Their bell was clearly not a
marvel, in sight nor sound. One glance told them the metals
had not bonded, for the dull-looking bell was full of cracks
and holes. The bell's sound promised to be even worse. At
best it might produce a muffled clang. Word of the failure
was reported immediately to the emperor.

The founders waited for imperial word, but there was
none. The emperor's silence was far more threatening than

the angry response they had feared. "Unless we are instructed otherwise, we shall meet back at the foundry in one week to begin again. Use this time to think well, for we will start with completely fresh minds," said Kuan-yu, "that is, unless we do not have our heads." And Kuan-Yu walked slowly home.

Ko-ai worried about her father. As she embroidered petals and blossoms on her wedding dress, she watched him pace up and down the garden path. Kuan-Yu looked so thin and old now. Ko-ai continued her work, embroidering willows and butterflies on her beautiful garment. When she looked up again, she saw her father sitting alone, rocking back and forth with worry.

"Oh, what am I to do?" he cried out to his daughter. "The wrath of the emperor shall soon be upon me, and you and your mother will live forever in disgrace."

And once again, the wise daughter offered him words of strength: "Fear not for me, nor for my mother. Put your thoughts to the bell. I believe all is possible through persistence and courage. The bell will be perfect. You will see, my father."

"Persistence and courage," Kuan-Yu chanted quietly to himself, as he walked the road to Peking next morning. With his spirits lifted, he once again met with the bell-founders. They discussed the previous casting and acknowledged some of the mistakes that may have been made. Some had new ideas for the bell, based on wisdom gleaned from consultations with magicians and scholars. Some had spoken to holy men and hermits to gain spiritual insight to the bell's preparation.

Once again, the emperor sent in piles of precious raw metals and a new mold was prepared to receive them. After a week of diligent work, the metals were melted and the court notified to attend the second casting of the Great Bell. At the sign of the emperor's waving fan and the stroke of the gong, the massive cauldron of molten bell metal was lifted and tilted. A golden cloud of steam filled the air as the cauldron was emptied. The emperor stared down at the earthen mold, then shifted his penetrating glance to Kuan-Yu. The old man shuddered, for in five days he would know his fate.

Sighs of deep despair again were heard. When the mold was lifted, the second bell stood duller in color and was studded with holes and grooves. Deep crevasses and cracks ran down one side. So far was it from perfection that Kuan-Yu left the room without speaking. He headed for his village home to await his fate.

When the emperor heard of the disastrous founding, his impatience turned swiftly to anger. "Such incompetence will be tolerated no longer," he declared, and sent for the court calligrapher to prepare a royal decree. It was dispatched immediately to Kuan-Yu.

Again the old man trembled at the sight of the yellow silk scroll with the red and golden dragon seal. He sank to the floor, his heart as heavy as if it had been cast in bronze. "I have not the strength to read this message of my doom."

Ko-ai ran to his side and said, "You must read it, Father." And together they unsealed the scroll and looked at the words printed there:

> Kuan-Yu, twice you have failed to cast the Great Bell of Peking. You have insulted the faith placed in you by the Son of Heaven. You have made a mockery of his trust. One more chance will be given you. Should you fail a third time, you shall die the death of a traitor. Fail, and your head will be severed from your body. Obey the commands of your emperor, or perish.

Ko-ai looked at her father. Great lines of pain and worry were etched into his once-smooth face, and his sheeny hair was now a dull white. "Oh, Ko-ai," he said, trembling, "I did not mean to bring disgrace to our family. When I am killed, the village will turn its back on you and your mother. You will be left no better than beggars. I cannot bear the thought. You, my dear Ko-ai, were to have worn your splendid golden orange garment; now you will be forced to wear the robe of disgrace."

"No, that never shall be," said Ko-ai. "You will make the perfect bell. You will see, my father." For Ko-ai had resolved to help him.

While Kuan-Yu was away at the foundry planning his third casting, Ko-ai took a piece of her best jade to seek help from the famous astrologer of Peking. She presented him with the gem as payment for his counsel. Ko-ai explained her father's impossible situation and the fear she felt for his life. The old man stroked his long thin beard, then consulted his star maps, ancient scrolls, and books of magic. After lengthy consideration, he looked up and said: "Alas, it is an inauspicious time and place for a mixing of gold with silver and brass. They simply cannot be wedded now, unless human blood and flesh is added. But this would be a gruesome sacrifice. A maiden, pure of heart and spirit, must join the metals in the crucible before all forces can meld in harmony. That is the only way."

Ko-ai could not have imagined such a grim answer. But it was an answer nonetheless. Her father would not be executed and her mother would not end her days in disgrace. Ko-ai returned home, telling no one of her visit to the astrologer. She went straight to her work, finishing the last branch of weeping willow on her saffron-colored silk. When her father returned home, she merely said, "The bell will be perfect. You will see, my father. And I want to be there tomorrow to see for myself your great moment of triumph."

The next morning Ko-ai went with her father to Peking. She wore her beautiful golden orange robe and she thought of all the dreams she had had while embroidering the intricate patterns on her dress and matching silk slippers.

In the foundry, she joined her father and the other founders, gathered on the large platform above the crucible. She looked into the swirling metal brewing beneath her. Her eye caught glints of gold, waves of red, and then suddenly all looked silvery white. The stern emperor waved his fan and the gong sounded. But before the cauldron could be lifted, Ko-ai moved forward on the platform and looked straight into the hissing liquid below. "You will have the perfect bell. You will see, my father," she called out, in a voice sweeter than that of the imperial nightingale. Ko-ai soared through the misty air, graceful as a golden butterfly with outstretched orange wings.

Ko-ai disappeared into the white-hot pool and the metal seemed to roar with satisfaction. Then the crucible lifted, for no one could stop the process, and spilled its contents into the mold. Her father moved to leap into the cauldron after his daughter, but was restrained by the other bellmakers. Kuan-Yu collapsed in grief. There at his side was his daughter's small embroidered slipper. He clutched the dainty shoe to his heart and wept bitterly. The old man was carried home by the emperor's guard and instructed to rest until summoned.

At the foundry many noted how much whiter and more glistening the metal appeared as it poured. "Like a silver fire dragon, the likes I have never before witnessed," ventured one of the senior founders. The mold was removed with great care and this time the sigh was one of immense relief. A cheering began, for the bell was a radiant color and perfect in form. The bell was hung and Kuan-Yu was brought to the imperial bell tower to witness its first tones.

He cared not to listen as he thought of his daughter's sacrifice. The Great Bell was struck and a deep and sonorous note sounded. The golden tone grew in splendor and vibrated through all who heard it. *Ko-ai*, it seemed to say, *Ko-ai*, then a sound like a silvery whisper followed.

"Hark," said the emperor. "Do you hear?" All listened attentively to the Great Bell.

Ko-ai, it rang again, and then came the silver sound like a hushed whisper: *hsieh*.

They knew what the bell was saying, for *hsieh* is the Chinese word for slipper. "It is my Ko-ai," said the father, with tears of joy. "She is crying out for her lost shoe."

Then the emperor bowed his head and all in his court followed his gesture. "Kuan-Yu," he declared, "you have created a bell of perfection for the great city of Peking.

And your daughter, Ko-ai, will forever be remembered and honored for giving the bell a soul."

At this the Great Bell of Peking sent out a resounding golden tone. *Ko-ai*, it rang, and the hundred little bells shook in happiness on the pagoda below the great tower. Then, *hsieh*, and one mother on the street below said: "Listen, my children, for dear Ko-ai is crying out for her slipper."

POOR SINNER

Long ago in Prussia, a bellmaker was assigned the duty of creating a bell of beautiful tone for the city's church. The bellmaker wanted everything to be perfect for the casting and took great pains in every stage of planning. He was an exacting and difficult man, as the young boy who had only recently started apprenticing at the foundry would find out.

On the morning the bell was to be cast, the bellmaker was summoned on emergency business to a neighboring village. He was most hesitant to leave the foundry at such a crucial time, but the matter was deemed urgent. Before leaving, he went over all vital instructions one last time with his young apprentice. "Remember," he cautioned, shaking a long bony finger at the petrified boy, "on no account are you to go near the furnace. The metals are now melting and by this afternoon when I return, we will cast the bell." The bell-maker put on his hat and coat, turning back one more time before leaving the foundry. "Remember what I have told you, boy. Do not touch anything. Your duty is only to keep the fires steady."

It was hot inside the foundry and the boy grew restless. With his stern master away, he began to fiddle and play with some of the tools left about. He looked over at the crucible suspended above the furnace and wondered how the metal was progressing. He had only started apprenticing and had never seen a bell being cast. He imagined the molten metal must be a strange and wild sight, streaming into the bell mold below.

The boy walked over to the furnace. He picked up a fireplace poker and tapped gingerly on the long pipe attached to the crucible. As he pulled the poker back, it caught on a small latch protruding from the side of the pipe. Immediately there was a great *hiss*, and a white spray of hot steam shot forth. The boy jumped back in alarm, only to watch in horror as a thick silvery white liquid oozed from the pipe. Slow at first, it soon began to pour in a steady stream. The boy leaned forward, trying to shut the latch, but the scorching heat made it impossible to move any nearer. Trembling as he watched the molten metal flow to fill the bell mold, the boy hung his head and began to weep.

At this dismal moment, the bellmaker returned to the foundry. His shouts alerted the boy, who turned to face his furious master. The bellmaker was enraged. The lad ran over to beg forgiveness, but before a word left his mouth the bellmaker struck him. The violent blow hit the boy's temple and the poor child fell to the floor, dead.

The man was horrified and picked up the body of the little apprentice. He ran through the streets like a madman, crying out for help. Over and over he swore he hadn't meant to hit the child so hard. "I struck out in anger," he explained. Although the bellmaker expressed remorse, he was brought to trial, found guilty of murdering his young apprentice, and sentenced to be hanged the next week.

As he sat in prison awaiting execution, the new bellmaker at the foundry discovered a bell cooling in the mold. He lifted it out and marveled at how perfectly it was cast. The bell was tested and all delighted in its clear ringing tone. They made arrangements to hang the bell in the church tower.

The very first occasion on which the bell rang was for an execution. It tolled as the old bellmaker was led through the streets and past the church tower. As he walked the last few steps to the gallows, the bell continued to sound the death knell.

Although the bell was given an official name – after the church in which it hung – the townspeople never did call it by its christened name. The church bell was forever known as Poor Sinner.

THE ROSE
AND CROWN

An old bell-founder had spent a whole day preparing for the moment he would cast the new village bell. Finally the furnaces were hot enough to melt down the broken pieces of metal. All had been added and the bellmaker realized there was not enough metal to fill the mold properly. He raced around the room, looking under tables and in bins, peering in every cupboard and shelf to find scrap metal he might add. The bell-founder began to panic, for he knew the melting process had reached a critical point, where all could be spoiled.

The villagers had saved for years for this bell and failure would be unforgivable. The old man rushed around the foundry one last time, looking for anything he could possibly melt down. Again, nothing. He grabbed a large sack, ran out of the foundry, and raced down the hill straight to the local pub. Bursting through the door without so much as a word of explanation, he began to grab pewter flagons and cooking pots, forks, knifes, spoons and anything metal that wasn't nailed down. He grabbed pewter goblets from customers before they could take their first sip. No one could say a word in protest, as they were all simply shocked at the raid. They watched incredulously as the old man stuffed every item into his sack and raced back out the door.

He ran up the hill, clanking and clattering all the way back to his foundry. There, he opened the sack and, with one toss, all the contents of the Rose and Crown were swallowed up by the molten bell metal.

Some still call the bell in the village square the Rose and Crown, and many a night at the pub, someone raises a glass to the memory of the old bellmaker whose fast thinking and wild tavern raid saved the day.

TING, TONG,
AND PLUFF

In a small village in rural England, three bells sound every Sunday morning to call the congregation to worship. Local folk know the distinct ringing anywhere, for there is no other peal quite so unique. "Hurry, children," cry mothers and fathers. "Ting, Tong, and Pluff are ringing. Hasten, or we shall be late." No one can recall quite when, but all know the story of how Ting, Tong, and Pluff came to be rung along that old country lane.

One early Sunday morning, many years ago, a man was walking through the English countryside. He was lost in thought, idly kicking a pebble along the dirt road as he strolled. At the sound of men shouting some distance away from him, he stopped for a moment. Squinting into the sun, he saw the figures of three men on a fence ahead, where the dirt road he was traveling on met up with another. "Whatever is all the yelling about?" he wondered, as he neared the three men.

He stopped to watch as they shouted to a couple of young fellows approaching from the other road. "Come to church, Thompson! Come to church, Brown!" they called out.

Next came three old women and again the shouts, although somewhat more refined in tone: "Come to church, dear ladies."

The traveler watched in fascination. Finally, after most of the morning congregation had passed and there was no sign of stragglers, the traveler sauntered up to the three sitting on the fence. "My good sirs," he began, "how far is it to church?"

And they answered. "Not far," said the first. "Not a quarter mile," added the second. "Round the bend in the road and you're there," said the third.

"Well then, good fellows, whatever are you doing out here on a Sunday morning, yelling so loudly for everyone to go to church? Surely the bells from the steeple can be heard such a short distance down the road."

The first replied, "The church has no bells." The second agreed, "No bells to call the people," and the third continued, "So we are the bells, you see, sir."

At this, the traveler threw back his head in laughter. "Why you must be hoarse from yelling and sore from sitting on the fence," he said, and he scratched his head in wonderment as he looked at the earnest, but absurd trio. "What you need are bells."

The first almost fell off the fence sputtering, "But the village is poor." The second grabbed hold of his friend, then said, "We could we never afford bells." "And," piped up the third, "there is no official bellmaker in our village."

"No, sir, we can never have bells," they said in unison.

"Consider this," the traveler continued. "If I were to pay for the bells myself, would you three able-looking fellows be willing to make them?"

This time, the first man did fall off the fence, dragging the other two with him. They looked up with foolish grins at the stranger. "We are craftsmen, after all. Making bells is something we should be able to figure out," said the first, so all three agreed they would try their best at crafting the village bells. "If you let us work as befits our trades," said the second man. "And pay us in advance for our efforts," added the third.

The traveler shook their hands to settle the deal, then opened his leather satchel and handed them a goodly sum to cover the cost. "And, fine sirs, I look forward to hearing those church bells ring next time I visit your village."

It was some years before the traveler returned to that countryside. As he walked along on that early Sunday

morning, he could only stare in amazement at the site ahead of him on the road. There, sitting on the same fence as years before, were the same three men. "Whatever are you doing out here now on a Sunday?" he asked. "You agreed to fashion bells for the village to ring folk to church. I paid you, believing your word."

"Oh, this we have done, as befits our trades, as you agreed upon yourself, kind sir." Whereupon the three men held up the bells they had crafted with materials from their trades and rang them with great pride. *Ting*, rang the first sharply. *Tong*, tapped the muffled second, and *Pluff*, sounded the quiet third bell. *Ting, Tong, Pluff*.

"I am a tinker," said the first man sharply. "I, a carpenter," mumbled the second. "And I," said the third and gentlest of the trio, "am a shoemaker."

The traveler smiled, then roared with laughter at his folly. And the three men on the fence rang once more for their benefactor. *Ting*, rang the tin bell. *Tong*, tapped the wooden one, and *Pluff* was the quiet sound of the leather bell.

And every Sunday morning, rain or shine, the church bells of that small village can be heard ringing down the country lane just before the dirt road meets another. *Ting, Tong, Pluff*, they call out humbly, but with as great conviction and faith as any bell of metal has ever been known to ring out.

CASTING FREEDOM:
THE LIBERTY BELL

Hushed the people's swelling murmur,
Whilst the boy cries joyously;
"Ring!" he's shouting, "ring, grandfather,
Ring! Oh, ring for Liberty!"
Quickly at the given signal
The old bellman lifts his hand.
Iron music through the land.
 – From *Franklin Fifth Reader*
   by George Stillman Hilliard, 1871

On July 8, 1776, the bell atop the State House tower in Philadelphia rang out joyously with one purpose – to call the citizens to witness the reading of the Declaration of Independence. From that historic day onward, the Liberty

Bell became the key symbol of American Independence and freedom.

Although the Liberty Bell was not designed specifically for this great occasion, every part of the bell's history had been leading to this important role in the story of American Independence. From how the bell was founded to its prophetic inscription, the Liberty Bell seemed destined to herald the birth of an independent nation.

The famed bell was originally designed to celebrate the fiftieth anniversary of a noble, though less grand-scale, vision of freedom – William Penn's Charter of Privileges. The Pennsylvania Assembly ordered the bell in the late autumn of 1751. It instructed the renowned English bellmakers of Whitechapel Foundry to cast a 2,000 pound bell. The Speaker of the Pennsylvania Assembly, a Quaker named Isaac Norris, chose a biblical quotation for the bell's inscription: "Proclaim Liberty throughout all the Land to all the Inhabitants thereof."

A 2,080 pound bell, composed mostly of copper, made the journey by ship to America, arriving at its new home on September 1, 1752. Norris noted: "The bell is come ashore & in good order . . . we have not yet try'd the sound."

There the bell remained for six months, waiting to be hung in the cupola of the State House in Philadelphia. Sometime during that winter, someone must have decided to try out the bell's sound. Whatever really happened is unknown, but a person, who did not understand the great care required when striking bell metal, must have hit the bell improperly, causing it to crack. On March 10, 1753, when the bell was hung and officially sounded, the crack along its one side was discovered. The Speaker of the Assembly noted: "I had the mortification to hear that it was cracked by a stroke of the clapper without any other viollence [sic] as it was hung up to try the sound."

Plans were made to send the bell back to England, but there was no room to take the cracked bell aboard on that voyage. Rather than wait, two Philadelphia bellmakers, John Pass and John Stow, were employed to recast the cracked bell. Pass and Stow melted down the bell, adding more copper to the mix – one and a half ounces for each pound of bell metal. When the new bell was cooled and ready, it was tested for sound. The results were less than favorable, and many blamed the additional copper for the irritating high-pitched *ting* the bell produced. Pass and Stow were teased and their bell became a joke. The two embarrassed founders broke up the bell and melted it down to try again.

This second recasting produced a more pleasant sounding bell and in June 1753, this bell was hung in the steeple of the State House. But there were still some who were not convinced the bell was acceptable, most notably Isaac Norris, who simply wrote: "We got our Bell new cast here and it has been used some time but tho some are of opinion it will do I Own I do not like it."

Norris's letter of complaint led to the ordering of a new bell from Whitechapel Foundry. Ironically, this new bell from England sounded no better than Pass and Stow's bell, and it was agreed to leave the recast bell where it was in the steeple.

Although it bore the biblical inscription, this bell was not yet called the Liberty Bell. In 1753, folk simply called it the State House Bell. It rang for the first time that August, before meetings of the Assembly. In the years before Independence, the State House Bell rang for all big events. Although it rang out when George III became king in 1760, relations between the colonies and England were strained. Protests were common amongst the colonists, especially over new taxes. The State House Bell chimed along in objection, often ringing all day long.

In 1764, when Benjamin Franklin headed for London to present the colonies' grievances to the Crown, the bell rang out in hope and expectation. But matters only became worse and, over the next few years, the bell chimed for townspeople to attend meetings to challenge such British impositions as the Stamp Act. The bell was muffled by placing a leather pad on the clapper whenever vessels carrying tax stamps sailed by. The bell tolled when the Sugar Act was repealed, and rang as ships sailed up the Delaware with what was called monopoly tea. When Paul Revere, a bellmaker and ringer himself, made his famous ride on horseback to Philadelphia, the State House Bell rang to call citizens to hear the news from Boston.

There was so much ringing at this time that the townsfolk who lived near the State House formed their own protest. They petitioned the Assembly to stop all the bell-ringing and complained that they were not only put out, but also "distressed (by all the) ringing of the great Bell in the Steeple."

The bell, however, would continue tolling and ringing for every major event fought in those years of struggle with the British. On April 25, 1775, when the State House Bell rang, over eight thousand people crowded outside the Assembly to hear the announcement of the Battle of Lexington and Concord. Those assembled were stirred to action and vowed to defend life and liberty. It was clear on that day that the bell had become the voice to call out the Revolution.

Ironically, the bell did not ring on the most important day in American history – July 4, 1776. While that was the day the Declaration of Independence was dated, it was also the day the document was sent to the printer. So the sounds of liberty first rang out in Philadelphia on July 8, 1776, when the Declaration could be first presented to the public. For the full hour between eleven o'clock and twelve noon, the bell rang to call the townspeople to the State House yard. When the bell quieted, John Nixon took the platform to read the Declaration of Independence. As he spoke the closing lines, the bell commenced ringing in the celebration.

There was no missing the greater significance of the bell's inscription: "Proclaim Liberty throughout all the Land to all the Inhabitants thereof." But the bell was so great a symbol of American liberty that it became unsafe to keep it in sight of the British forces advancing toward Philadelphia in 1777. As they neared, Philadelphians removed the "Liberty" Bell from the steeple on September 11, fearful the British would capture it and melt it down for arms and ammunition. The bell was spirited away under guard, to be hidden under the floorboards of a church in nearby Allentown. There it remained until late in 1778, when it was returned to Philadelphia, but it was not rehung until the State House steeple was rebuilt in 1785.

The bell continued to ring in important events and celebrations for the next six decades. It tolled at the deaths of Benjamin Franklin, John Adams, and Thomas Jefferson. No one is certain exactly when the Liberty Bell cracked or how it happened, but it may have occurred in 1835. An eighty-six-year-old man named Emmanuel Rauch told his boyhood account of how and when the bell cracked to a reporter in

1911. In the story that appeared in the *Sunday New York Times* on July 16, 1911, Rauch claimed that in 1835, when he was ten years old, the steeple keeper at the State House asked Rauch and several of his friends if they might like to ring the bell for Washington's birthday. Major Jack Downing, the steeple keeper, then tied a rope to the clapper of the bell and gave the other end to Rauch and the boys. They were told to pull down with all their might, and so they did. But after about a dozen strokes, the sound above them changed. Immediately, Downing raced up into the steeple. There he saw the dreadful reason for the change of tone. It was a thin crack, but one that ran well over a foot in length. Downing, realizing his folly, ordered the boys to leave.

There are several other theories on how this crack first appeared, but one thing is known for sure. When the bell was last rung on Washington's birthday in 1846, that ringing expanded the crack to its present-day "zigzag" version. The account in the Philadelphia public ledger on February 26, 1846 describes this ringing of the Liberty Bell:

The old Independence Bell rang its last clear note on Monday last in honor of the birthday of Washington and now hangs in the great city steeple irreparably cracked and dumb. It had been cracked before but was set in order of that day by having the edges of the fracture filed so as not to vibrate against each other . . . It gave out clear notes and loud, and appeared to be in excellent condition until noon, when it received a sort of compound fracture in a zigzag direction through one of its sides which put it completely out of tune and left it a mere wreck of what it was.

Although the Liberty Bell appeared "a mere wreck of what it was," its power as a national symbol has remained intact. It is a reminder of American Independence to the over one million people who view it every year. Until 1925 it was displayed in a glass case, but so many people made requests to touch the bell, the case was removed.

Throughout its history, the Liberty Bell has traveled to world fairs. In 1915 it was one of the featured exhibits at the Panama-Pacific Exposition in San Francisco, California. Along the train route west, the bell was greeted by marching bands, waving flags, and gun salutes. When the Liberty Bell finally came home, it was paraded through the streets of Philadelphia.

America's bicentennial celebrations in 1976 made special provisions for the Liberty Bell. To accommodate the over one million people who were traveling to Philadelphia each year to see the Liberty Bell, it was given its own special pavilion on Independence Mall. On July 4, 1976, it was ceremonially rung, tapped with a specially made mallet, to celebrate two hundred years of liberty.

The spirit of the Liberty Bell has been celebrated by Americans throughout their country's history. It remains an inspirational symbol of liberty and justice for all.

RINGING OUT
LIBERTY

A picture of the bell appeared in an 1837 publication called Liberty, *put out by the New York Anti-Slavery Society. The bell became a strong symbol for the abolition- ist movement and appeared for the first time as the Liberty Bell in a poem of the same title in a Boston abolitionist pamphlet. The poem "The Liberty Bell" found a greater audience when it was reprinted in another anti-slavery publication,* The Liberator.

Since that time, the Liberty Bell has rung out to proclaim liberty. When the Allied forces landed in France on June 6, 1944, the Liberty Bell's tones were broadcast throughout the nation. A special D-Day radio broadcast featured the bell as the voice of freedom ringing out. The Liberty Bell sounded twelve times to signify independence and another seven times at the show's end to symbolize liberty. Since the cracked bell could not be rung, a special rubber mallet was designed so the bell could be tapped safely.

Other freedom groups have gathered strength of purpose from the bell over the years. A replica of the Liberty Bell became a guiding symbol for the women's suffrage movement. The group called their bell the Women's Liberty Bell, or the Justice Bell. To symbolize their struggle, the bell's clapper was chained and could not be sounded. The chain was to be removed only when American women were given a voice in politics, with the right to vote. The suffrage leader, Katherine Ruschenberger, stated the group's intent in a *New York Times* article in March 1915: "The original Liberty Bell announced the creation of democracy; the Women's Liberty Bell will announce the completion of democracy." The Women's Liberty Bell was unchained and rung with the passing of the Nineteenth Amendment in 1919.

The bell became a symbol for African Americans again in the 1960s when civil rights protesters held a "sit-in" around the Liberty Bell. The purpose of the demonstration was to focus attention on the need to protect the rights of African Americans in Alabama.

In a symbolic gesture acknowledging liberty and independence, the bell's original foundry, Whitechapel in England, cast the Bicentennial Bell in 1976. The inscription reads:

For the people of the United States of America
From the people of Britain
4 July 1976
Let freedom ring

CASTING PEACE
INTO WAR

Die Glocken kämpfen mit für ein neues Europa!
The bells join a fight for a new Europe.
— Nazi slogan during World War II

Tin and copper are the metals of bells. They are also the metals of cannons. In wartime, bells are silenced – their ringing metals transformed by fire into blasting cannons.

Bells have always been prized by conquering armies. They were officially seized upon victory, removed from their towers, melted down, and recast into arms. Napoleon made this practice part of his code of operations.

During World War II, the Nazis ordered over 150,000 bells to be taken from European towers and melted down for battle use. Even when metals were not needed, the

Nazis wanted bells removed to prevent them falling into Allied hands.

V

BELLS
THE WHOLE
DAY LONG:
THE RHYTHM
OF LIFE

DICK WHITTINGTON AND THE BELLS OF BOW

Many centuries ago in England, in the reign of King Edward III, there lived a boy named Dick Whittington. For as long as young Dick could remember, he had been alone in the world. Both his parents died when he was a baby and he was without any relatives to look after him. From little up, he had taken care of himself. Dick wandered the English countryside doing farm chores in exchange for food and shelter. "That child is as wild as a young wolf, but a smart and kindly boy he seems to be," one farmer noted to his wife. Many a person asked Dick to stay on to help with the daily work, but Dick always replied that he was heading down the road to see what fortune might lie round the bend.

One day, as Dick was walking a narrow country lane, he heard the ringing of bells coming from behind him. He turned around, then from a cloud of dust, a wagon appeared.

"Which way are you headed, young fellow?" the wagoner called out to Dick.

And Dick, who was really going nowhere in particular but did not like to admit his aimlessness, replied, "Why, I am going to where the road ends."

"Well, fancy that, my boy," laughed the peddler, "that's just where I am headed too – London town."

All his young life, Dick Whittington had heard about London town. Country folk he had met in his travels told him, in hushed voices, of the splendor of the big city. In London, he heard tell, the streets were paved with pure gold. Everyone was wealthy, for once one walked the golden cobblestones, luck was always at his heels.

"It's a long and dangerous walk so late in the day," continued the peddler. "My wagon is loaded, but you may walk beside it for safety's sake."

Dick had often wished to see the great glittering city. Now that his chance had come, he suddenly felt afraid. Yet he answered, "I will be most relieved to walk alongside your wagon," for, when he thought about it, there was really no reason to stay behind in the countryside.

Dick walked alongside the wagon at a brisk pace. He was not tired, for each step excited him with the thought of nearing the wondrous city where everyone sang and danced on streets of gold. Surely fortune was now to be his. The young boy, who had only ever known a meager living, imagined himself as a famous gentleman, living in great wealth. His pace quickened.

Dick and the wagoner entered the center of London town just as the sun was setting. The boy gasped at the marvelous sites, for in the early evening light of sunset the streets appeared to glow an orangey gold. The church spires and roofs of the neighboring estates also caught the dazzling light. "A city where all is gold," thought Dick, and he thanked the wagoner, then headed off.

By now Dick was exhausted and he curled up in the back of a laneway to rest. "First thing tomorrow, I will break a small bit of gold off one of the cobblestones and have enough money for at least a month's fine living," mumbled the tired boy as he drifted off to sleep, a happy smile on his lips.

When he awoke next morning, Dick could not believe his eyes. "I must still be asleep," he thought, "surely this is a bad dream." Where, the night before, he had seen streets paved in gold, he now saw dull and muddied cobblestone strewn with filth. Dick raced to the end of the laneway, hoping he had somehow wandered off the main golden roadway, but there ahead of him was more dirty gray stone.

Sadly he realized the bleak and horrible truth of his situation. He had come all this way on a fool's dream. Now he was walking the grimy city streets, with neither money in his pockets nor food. He needed to find work immediately, but here in the city his worn country clothes looked no better than those of the beggars and street urchins who hung about in the dark alleys. The fine people of London glanced at him with suspicious eyes, as if he might rob them as he passed by.

After a day of wandering the streets hoping to find employment, Dick sat down on the cold cobblestone, hungry and desperate. He begged passersby for a penny to buy a loaf of bread. A boot kicked him hard in the leg and then again in the ribs. "Move away from my stand, you wretched waif. Why don't you work for a living?" yelled the man. He struck Dick a swift blow to the head as the boy was standing up. "Come on now, be off with you."

Dick hung his head low as he stumbled away from the market square. "What a fool I've been," he cried to himself. "How I wish I had stayed in the countryside, where you can at least find straw to sleep in." As darkness fell on the city, Dick came to a fine house. He fell to his knees, sobbing and bleeding, and huddled in the dark shelter of the doorway. There the wretched boy fell fast asleep and that is where the owner of the fine house, Mr. Fitzwarren, found poor Dick Whittington the next morning.

Mr. Fitzwarren was one of London's most successful merchants. He was about to call a servant to remove the unkempt boy from his doorstep, when he noticed the sleeping lad's face. There he saw a gentleness and sweetness of nature. "Poor sweet boy," said Mr. Fitzwarren, and he shook Dick lightly by the shoulder to wake him. "Your name, young fellow? Tell me to whom you belong."

"My name is Dick Whittington and I am an orphan. I know not a soul in London, sir." At this Dick began to sob.

"Come along, Dick," said Mr. Fitzwarren, "my cook shall prepare you a fine meal and get you clean clothing."

"You have been the first to show me kindness, sir. Thank you," said Dick, whose eyes welled up, this time with tears of joy.

Mr. Fitzwarren smiled at the boy. "Dick Whittington, you shall work for me." He introduced him to the cook and instructed her to look after Dick's needs, then show him to his chores.

All would have been well with Dick had it not been for the cook. She was a nasty and unhappy woman who bossed the boy from morning to night. Nothing Dick did pleased her and he spent most of his days dodging the swing of her ladle or her broomstick. "Don't smudge the silverware;

polish it, I said," she would yell, or, "Bring in the wood and don't be so slow, you idiotic boy."

Once, Mr. Fitzwarren's daughter, Alice, came into the kitchen just as the cook was threatening to cut off one of Dick's ears with a kitchen knife. Alice came to the boy's defense, giving the cook a stern warning. From that point on, the cook was careful whenever she knew Mistress Alice was about. So, for a time, Dick had some relief.

But each night, after a day of scrubbing floors and washing dishes, the boy retired to his bed, high up in the garret. As soon as he blew out his candle, he heard the sound he had come to dread – first a scurry from the rafters over-head, then a squeaking. Dick shut his eyes and pulled the threadbare quilt up over his face. He prepared for the next sensation – dozens of little feet scampering over his covered body, nibbling at the bedclothes and mattress. Every night was the same. The attic was full of rats and mice.

One morning, after a particularly troublesome night with rats, Dick was clearing trays from the dining room just as a guest was arriving. The gentleman asked Dick to brush his shoes before his meeting with Mr. Fitzwarren. This Dick did, and was promptly paid a penny.

The next day Dick saw a girl walking by with a cat under her arm. He ran out the door, yelling, "A penny for your cat. I'll give you a penny." When she shook her head *no*, Dick implored her, explaining he had no other money and that his need for the feline was indeed great.

"Fine, you may have her," the girl said. "I promise you she is an extraordinary mouser."

Dick snuck up the back staircase with Puss, for that is what he called the cat. He was frightened of what the cook might do if she found out and whispered, "Listen here, Puss, you'll have plenty of mice to hunt, only don't *meow* too loudly, for if you're found here by the cook, you'll be booted out the door or even worse." And he closed the door at the bottom of the garret stairs.

Puss proved to be an extraordinary mouser, ever ready for a good chase and fearless, even when she faced down rats almost as big as herself. Dick stroked his ginger-colored cat, rewarding her with scraps from the cook's leftovers. At least now, Dick could get a peaceful night's sleep.

Not long after, Mr. Fitzwarren called all of his servants together in his study to make what had become his annual speech: "As you know, I am a merchant who has made a fine living from the riches of trade. Again this year, I have reserved a space in the ship's hold for any goods or valuables you may wish to trade. My gift to you, as a yearly bonus, is shipment with neither freight nor taxes to pay. All monies received from objects sold will go directly to the owner. The boat leaves tomorrow for the Barbary Coast. May each of you find prosperity in this transaction."

As always, there was great excitement. Most servants already knew what they would part with, and brought it with them to the gathering. Dick walked away, certain he had nothing to offer. Alice spotted him leaving and spoke up to her father: "Dick Whittington has no worldly goods to send. Allow me to make a donation on his behalf, Father."

But Mr. Fitzwarren was adamant: "The donation must come from Dick himself, if he is to profit."

Dick, hearing the family discussion, spoke up: "Thank you, Miss Alice, but it is fine. I have no worldly possession but for my cat."

"Well go fetch that cat, Dick," said Mr. Fitzwarren, "and she will travel the seven seas." But Dick did not want to part with his cat. For all her mousing prowess, he had simply grown fond of her company. "Go fetch the cat now, or she will not make the shipment."

With tears in his eyes, Dick handed over Puss. And Alice gave him a penny to buy another mouser.

As the ship left the next morning, the miserable cook looked at Dick and smirked. "Listen, boy," she taunted, "I wouldn't get my hopes set too high. After all, what can an old fleabag be worth to anyone? I hope that cat of yours has sea legs." And she laughed and threw more of her ill-tempered comments at poor Dick: "I wondered where some of the scraps had disappeared to these past few weeks and now I see all too clearly," and she gave Dick a great *whack* with the wooden ladle. "You're nothing but an idiot, Dick Whittington."

That night, Dick sat alone in his garret room and stared out toward the harbor, to the sea where Puss was heading off to foreign lands. She had been his one faithful friend and Dick had told her his great hopes. Finally he broke down – "I'm just so lonely without my cat" – and all the injustices of the cook's harsh treatments swept through his mind. "Tomorrow, I'm going to leave London for good," he determined.

Dick got up very early with a great resolve to depart. It was the morning of All Hallow's Eve and Dick set out at a fast clip, so to be well out of London before evening. He did not dare to stop until he was far away from Mr. Fitzwarren's house. He would miss his master and Miss Alice, but life there had been too hard. Dick walked all the way to Highgate Hill, on the outskirts of the city, before he stopped to rest. There he sat down on a stone and looked out over the city he had left behind.

Just then, the sound of church bells filled the air. "The Bells of Bow," thought Dick and he fancied the six bells were chiming a farewell to him. Dick was about to get up and continue on, when the bells caught his attention again. This time they sounded slightly different. He listened closely and was shocked when the bells seemed to be talking. Dick heard a message; it was definitely for him: "Turn again, Whittington. Thrice Lord Mayor of London."

"What is the meaning of the bells' message?" the stunned lad wondered aloud. "Turn again must mean to turn around and go back to London," he surmised. As for the part about thrice Lord Mayor, Dick felt sure it must mean he would be elected Lord Mayor of London three times. "Lord Mayor of London!" Dick muttered to himself with satisfaction. He had always felt in his heart that he would be a great man, and now the bells had told him so.

So Dick turned around and headed back to Mr. Fitzwarren's employment. "If I am to be Lord Mayor of London, surely I can endure the cook for a little while longer. I will not miss my great chance because of an ill-tempered old woman." Dick was now feeling confident. "I will only laugh at her and tell her she doesn't know who she is really hitting," he mused. And, with great spirit in each step, Dick ran all the way back to London town, in time for the evening meal.

Now and then, Dick looked out on the city harbor and wondered how Puss was faring on the open seas. In fact, Mr. Fitzwarren's ship was sailing along at a fine clip, favorable winds blowing the whole way. At last it came up the Barbary Coast and made port in an exotic kingdom. No sooner had

the crew put down anchor, than the king of that country
sent his messengers down to the ship to bid the strangers
welcome and to invite the captain and the ship's business
agent to dine at the Imperial Palace.

That evening the two officials arrived, eager to dine
with the king and queen. What splendor awaited them! Rich
tapestries hung from every wall, marbled pillars lined the
hallways, gold silken carpets covered the floors, and there in
the center of a great room stood the banquet table. The
captain and the agent were presented to the imperial couple,
then seated at the large table. But no sooner had the servants
brought in the first course of delicacies, than the entire table
was covered with rats. The rodents jumped upon the food,
quickly devouring most of the feast. They were bold and
furious varmints. Not even the work of seven full-time
rat-catching guards could arrest the attack. As fast as one rat
was dealt with, another two appeared.

Mr. Fitzwarren's agent looked aghast. "Has this ever
happened before, Your Majesty?" he asked.

"At every meal," said the king, "and I swear I would give
much of the kingdom's treasure to be free of these vermin."

"Do you truly mean that?" checked the agent.

"Absolutely," was the monarch's quick reply, "for my
wife, the queen, loses much sleep over these rodents. Even
with a guard posted outside our sleeping chamber, the rats
still manage to get in and run up and down the royal canopy.

My wife has not had a full night's sleep for many a moon. Yes, I would gladly pay a great amount of gold and jewels to be rid of the whole ugly lot."

"Your Royal Highness," said the captain, "if you will excuse me, I have a solution aboard our ship – a creature who will catch each and every one of those rodents. If you will allow my agent leave, I assure you that you and the queen will be well pleased."

The queen smiled and the king dismissed the agent with one finger. "Oh, do run. I am impatient to see this wondrous creature," said the queen. At this the agent headed off at a great clip straight for the cabin, where he knew Puss would be sleeping.

An hour later the agent returned with a biscuit bag in his hand – a bag that appeared to be moving of its own accord. "Is the great mouse-hunting creature in that bag?" asked the queen nervously.

The agent loosened the bag's drawstrings just as the servants were setting a feast of sweets on the banquet table. An army of mice and rats pounced on the delicacies and an orange flash streaked across the room. In an instant, Puss had put an end to the rodents. Many lay dead on the floor and the rest fled in panic.

So impressed was the king, he made an offer to the agent that could not be refused: "I will buy all the goods in your cargo hold for whatever price you ask and give you ten times that for this magnificent rodent-catching beast." A handshake settled the deal and the king expressed his delight at the bargain.

Just before the ship departed, the queen sent twelve more barrels filled with gold and jewels for the previous owner of the beast, as she had already become fond of the new pet she called Puddy. "Puddy will be well cared for. Already she sleeps on Her Highness's lap when she tires from her mousing" was the official word from the palace.

Several months later, the merchant ship arrived back in London town. Mr. Fitzwarren was up early that morning, at work in his countinghouse, when a loud rap on the door disturbed his calculations. Angrily, he opened the door. There stood the captain and in the hallway were great barrels spilling over with gems and gold. The captain explained the great fortune paid for the cargo and for Dick Whittington's cat. "Surely you will give the boy but a fraction of the treasure, sir," suggested the captain, "for he could not be trusted to handle so great a fortune."

But Mr. Fitzwarren shook his head and shouted: "Fetch the boy, Dick Whittington, and bring him to the countinghouse at once. He shall have his due down to the penny and all shall be happy for his prosperity."

When Dick arrived, he could not meet his master's eyes, sure he had been summoned to be ridiculed about sending a lowly cat to sea. But he could not believe his ears when he heard his master's words: "Dear Whittington, I congratulate you on your great fortune. Look here at what the sale of your cat has brought you." Dick could scarcely believe his eyes. Immediately he gave a handful of jewels to each of the servants, including the cook.

"See that young Whittington is treated like the proper gentleman he is," Mr. Fitzwarren instructed his chief servant. "Have him bathed, then call in the barber and London's best tailor."

When Dick entered for dinner that night, Mistress Alice was much pleased by the transformation. She realized that he was indeed a most handsome young man. The merchant noticed the two staring at each other across the table during dinner and proposed a match right there on the spot. The two could not hide their happiness and Dick presented Alice with a string of pearls to wear around her slender neck.

After dinner, the master made another proposal: "Let us trade together, Whittington. Together our fortunes will grow." And Dick, who respected the merchant greatly, agreed to the partnership. "And when I die," added the merchant, "you shall be my heir."

Dick married Alice Fitzwarren and went on to become an even richer man. The young family prospered. Dick worked diligently and was a well-liked merchant, known to the people as Richard Whittington. He soon became Lord

Mayor of London. As he paraded through the city streets in the Lord Mayor's coach, Dick heard the great bells clanging high above him. Their sound reminded him of the Bells of Bow, which had spoken to him so many years before. "Turn again, Whittington. Thrice Lord Mayor of London."

Dick sat still in his coach, listening to the ringing. He remembered the ragged homeless young boy he had been and the charity he had received in those early days. As he listened to the bells, he felt humbled by the resounding reminder, and Dick resolved to use his power and money to help the unfortunate. For years, Lord Mayor Richard Whittington built churches, hospitals, and colleges. He fed the poor and funded aspiring scholars, so they might better their lives.

And true to the prophetic song of the Bells of Bow, Dick Whittington became Lord Mayor of London – not once, but three times. In his last year as Lord Mayor, he was knighted for his noble actions. When Sir Richard Whittington died at a fine old age, he was greatly mourned and lovingly remembered. For Dick Whittington had never forgotten his humble beginnings. In his will, he bequeathed large sums of money for "pore young beginners," widows, aged men, and young scholars.

Dick Whittington also remembered the bells in his will. He left money to pay for the ringing of the "Tenor Bell of Bow Church every morning at six o'clock and every evening at eight." People who live in the part of London where the bell can still be heard call themselves Cockneys. They say they were born within the sound of the Bells of Bow and never a day passes that the bells do not remind them of the poor boy, Dick Whittington, who rose to great fortune in the city. Some follow his famous walk to the point halfway up Highgate Hill to consider their fortune on "Whittington's Stone."

THE POETRY
OF STEEPLES

England has been dubbed the Ringing Isle because of its many churches and bells. For centuries, the sound of bells has accompanied life in cities and towns, giving a rhythm to the workings of the day. Each bell has its own peculiar tone and people have always fancied words and rhymes to match the ringing. There are hundreds of these short verses for bells all over the Ringing Isle.

"Oranges and Lemons" is an entire poem made of these bell rhymes. It is often sung as a nursery rhyme, but children also play it as a game. "Oranges and Lemons" is also known as "The Merrie Bells of London," as it names the city's churches and gives a sense of what the neighborhoods were like throughout the London of days gone by. Was the bell-ringing heard in a part of the city where fancy carriages paraded up and down cobblestone streets, or was this

a bell-ringing where blacksmiths worked over hot fires with pokers and tongs, and vendors walked through the streets with their wares of kettles and pans?

Oranges and Lemons
or
The Merrie Bells of London

Gay go up and gay go down,
To ring the bells of London town:
Oranges and lemons,
Say the bells of St. Clement's.

Pancakes and fritters,
Say the bells of St. Peter's.
Bulls' eyes and targets,
Say the bells of St. Marg'ret's.
Brickbats and tiles,
Say the bells of St. Giles'.
Two sticks and an apple,
Say the bells of Whitechapel.
Old Father Baldpate,
Say the slow bells of Aldgate.
Maids in white aprons,
Say the bells of St. Catherine's.
Pokers and tongs,
Say the bells of St. John's.
Kettles and pans,
Say the bells of St. Anne's.
Halfpence and farthings,
Say the bells of St. Martin's.
You owe me ten shillings,
Say the bells of St. Helen's.
When will you pay me?
Say the bells of Old Bailey.
When I grow rich,
Say the bells of Shoreditch.
Pray, when will that be?
Say the bells of Stepney.

I do not know,
Says the great bell at Bow.
Here comes a candle to light you to bed,
And here comes a chopper to chop off your head.

OUTSIDE
LONDON TOWN

Northern, sweet music,
And Didsbury pans;
Cheadel old kettles,
And Stockport old cans.
  – Of four churches near Manchester

O utside of London are all sorts of variations of these couplets and stories about what people hear the bells saying. There are even places where the bells are thought to have conversations with out-of-town bells. In one village the bells cry out: "Who rings best? Who rings best?" To which the bells from the neighboring village call back: "We do, we do!"

The Bells of Burton used to ring a challenge across the Trent River to the Bells of Luddington: "Who rings best?

Who rings best?" And always, the Bells of Luddington would clearly answer: "We two, we two!"

Wharf Bells

The six bells in Derby rang out news of the day's catch at the wharves. "Fresh fish just come to town," they called out. The Bell of St. Michael had only this comment: "They stinken." And the Bells of All Saints' Cathedral tolled out advice: "Then put a little more salt on them."

Soccer Bells

Football fans heard their village bells ring out the following game:

Pancakes and fritters, say All Saints' and St. Peter's.
When will the ball come? say the bells of St. Alkmun'.
At two they will throw, say Saint Weabo.
Oh! Very well, says little Michael.

Shropshire Bell Rhymes

Wristle, wrastle,
Say the bells of Bishop's castle.

Hop, skip, and run,
Say the bells of Clun.
An owl in the tree,
Say the bells of Norbury.
Itchy and scabby,
Say the bells of the Abbey.
Three silver pickles,
Say the bells of St. Michael's.
Three golden canaries,
Say the bells of St. Mary's.
A boiling pot and stewing pan,
Say the bells of St. Julian.
Ivy, holly, and mistletoe,
Say the bells of Wistanstow.

THE RUNNING
OF THINGS

*One sound rose ceaselessly above the noises of busy life and
lifted all things into a sphere of order and serenity, the
sound of bells.*
　　　　　　　　　– Johan Huizinga

I n Europe in the Middle Ages, the Angelus Bell rang
from every community church tower at six o'clock in
the morning. Its rings were to remind all who heard to
bow their heads for a moment of grateful prayer. So
important was this bell considered to be for successful
praying that in small communities without a church, one
citizen was sent to the outskirts of town to listen for the
Angelus, then to run back ringing a handbell to announce
its message to all. The Angelus would sound two more times
during the day – at noon and in the evening.

Over time, the morning Angelus became the signal for the beginning of the town's day. Folk then rang out gate bells, and the mighty doors to the town were opened. The streets filled with merchants and peddlers with their carts, but no one could start the day's business until the Common Bell rang to announce the opening of the market. This was according to a law set out in 1478: "It is ordyred that no person opyn their sack or set ther corn to sale afore the hour of ten of the bell or els the undernone bell be rongyn."

Arise and go about your business.
– St. Ives bell inscription

On market days, the town square was full of stalls and, on special fair days, merchants from afar could join the regular market for a town fair. There were bells rung throughout the business day, with specialty bells announcing each vendor's wares. Simple Simon would have rung a pie bell, and the Muffin Man would have shaken a handbell up and down Drury Lane. Fishmongers, tool sharpeners, tinkers, and flower sellers all rang bells. So did the craftsmen in their guilds. The tanners and goldsmiths, the weavers and blacksmiths had bells that rang above their shop doors.

All legal transactions had to be completed within the specified hours of business. The Common Bell, or Market Bell, determined the opening and closing of the business day.

The Common Bell also served as a work bell to alert laborers to the beginning and end of their tiresome days.

> *I ring at six to let men know*
> *When to and from their worke to goe.*
>   – Coventry bell inscription, 1675

The apprentices and craftsmen in the area of London called Cheapside listened every morning at six o'clock for the Bow Bells to start their day, and then again at eight o'clock to end the day. Watches and clock chimes were rarities to most of the workers living there and the Common Bell was a real necessity. Once, all the apprentices were late for work and blamed the clerk, the ringer of the Bow Bells, for tardy ringing. The lively exchange between the two parties is preserved in verse:

> *Clerk of the Bow Bell*
> *With the yellow locks,*
> *For thy late ringing*
> *Thy head shall have knocks.*

> Children of Cheap,
> Hold you all still,
> For you shall hear the Bow Bell
> Rung at your will.

Bells regulated and brought order to the daily affairs of every town and city. There was the Oven Bell, the Butter Bell, the Dykes and Drains Jury Bell. There were racing peals and, in some European cities, the Bull-running Bell. More common ringing for festivities included wedding bells, Maypole peals, town fair bells, and the All-Hallows Bell.

Each community had a town crier who walked through the streets ringing a large handbell. His ringing called attention to an announcement about to be made. When he stopped at the street corner, he rang the handbell three times, then followed with a loud and hearty shout of "Oyes, oyes." When the crowd was listening, the town crier read his news, which could be anything from a government order, a report of a lost or stolen article, or notification of a reward.

The end of the city's workday was marked by the final Angelus and the ringing of the Common Bell. The laws of York in 1390 stated it was illegal for cooks throughout the city to purchase any supplies "between the evensong ringing of St. Michael's and the prime strike in the morning."

A bell at the close of day brought all activity to an end and the city gates were closed for the night. In Flanders, this last bell came to be known as the Thieves Bell, as many robbers left the city at the first ringing. They were locked safely outside the city gates with the stolen property. In one city, tales were told of thieves who tried to escape with their goods after the gate was closed by swimming across the moat. The clever guardsman had set a trap in the water, though. A net with many small bells attached was strung across the moat and when the thieves tried to escape, they were given away by the ringing of the moat bells.

THE CURFEW
BELL

The curfew tolls the knell of parting day
       – From "Elegy in a Country Churchyard"
   by Thomas Gray, 1750

In the olden days, fire was the greatest threat to a town. Danger was constant, as every house kept a fire burning all day long. To make matters worse, these wooden houses were built close together. One un-attended fire, or even a shooting spark, could catch the entire village on fire as the flames leaped from one thatched-roof dwelling to the next.

One safety practice developed in ninth-century France. Villages decided to cover all fires for the night at an agreed time. The sounding of a late evening bell became the signal to smother the flames with a large metal lid called a *couvre-feu* (cover fire). The tradition developed that every evening, usually by nine o'clock, the bell rang to remind folk to extinguish their fires with the couvre-feu.

The idea came to England in 1066 with William the Conqueror. Over time, the French phrase became Anglicized and couvre-feu became curfew. The sounding of the Curfew Bell brought activities to a close. All fires were covered with ashes, and lights were put out. This blackout was perhaps the main reason William wanted the bell to be rung each night. A bell that required flames to be put out also meant no conspirators and troublemakers could linger about to plot treacherous acts against him.

Villages developed rules around the ringing of the Curfew Bell. In 1291, no wine was allowed to be served in some villages after the Curfew Bell, and pubs closed their doors for the night. The bell was also rung when political upheaval called for the quieting of evening activities. For these reasons, the ringing of the Curfew Bell was an unpopular sound. Folk no longer thought of its original beneficial reason for being, rather the Curfew Bell became a symbol of restraint and strict authority.

THE PANCAKE
BELL

But hark, I hear the pancake bell,
And fritters make a gallant smell.
The cooks are baking, frying, broiling,
Stewing, mincing, cutting, boiling,
Carving, gormandizing, roasting,
Carbonating, cracking, slashing, toasting.
      – From *Poor Robin's Almanac,* 1684

Shrove Tuesday, the day before Lent, is also called
Pancake Day. In Medieval England, Shrove Tuesday
was the day housewives went through the larder
gathering up all the eggs, fat, suet, and milk so they
would be used up before the forty strict days of Lent began.
The simplest recipe using this combination of ingredients was

pancakes, and the women scurried about to make a colossal batch before the Shriving Bell, or Pancake Bell, was rung.

At the sounding of the Pancake Bell, the largest of the church bells, all village activity came to a halt. Businesses closed and schoolmasters shut their books. The whole community headed to church to confess their sins and receive absolution before Lent began. After church, villagers went home to eat their stacks of pancakes. Everyone in the household, including servants and apprentices, sat at the table together to delight in their last fatty meal.

Many traditions have developed in England around the ringing of the Pancake Bell. The people of Olney hold a pancake race. The idea for the pancake race is thought to have originated years ago when one housewife was hurrying about, trying to fry all her pancakes before the Pancake Bell sounded. She was still cooking when it rang, but she needed to confess her sins before Lent. As the bell rang, she dashed out of her house toward the church, still holding the frying pan with its pancake. As she ran, the pancake was tossed out of the pan and back in again several times. Today's race in Olney has become a big event. All women over sixteen years old may take part in the 415-yard dash. All they need do is carry a frying pan with a pancake as they run. The tricky part is that all pancakes must be flipped in the air at least three times during the race and, of course, land safely back in the pan. The winner of the race receives a kiss from the pancake bellringer and a book of prayer from the vicar.

In Somerset the congregation gathers after the Pancake Bell to join hands in a gigantic circle that surrounds the church. This Pancake Day ritual is known as church clipping.

All over England the Pancake Bell signaled a last day of merriment, especially for apprentices and schoolchildren. Along with the feast of pancakes, there were often football games. The Pancake Bell was rung at twelve noon and, in some towns, it was a signal to schoolchildren for the "barring-out" (the locking out of their teachers from the classroom).

In Scarborough there is a two hundred-year-old tradition still observed by schoolchildren. At the sound of the Pancake Bell, they all race to the shore to skip. No matter what the weather on Shrove Tuesday, everyone – children and their parents – get out their ropes and skip.

Many English schoolchildren went a-shroving at the sound of the Pancake Bell. To go a-shroving meant going around the village, knocking on people's doors. When a neighbor opened the door, the children would sing a pancake song, or recite a verse. In payment for the entertainment, the neighbor would give them a piece of pancake and sometimes money.

Knock, knock, the pan's hot
And we are coming a-shroving
For a piece of pancake

Or a piece of truckle cheese
Of your making.

Tippety, tippety tin,
Give me a pancake and I will come in.
Tippety, tippety toe,
Give me a pancake and I will go.
       – Two traditional a-shroving verses

THE EXECUTION
BELL

All you that in the condemned hold do lie,
Prepare you, for tomorrow you shall die.
Watch all, and pray, the hour is drawing near
That you before the Almighty must appear;
Examine well yourselves, in time repent,
That you may not in eternal flames be sent,
And when St. Sepulchre's bell tomorrow tolls,
The Lord have mercy on your souls.
Past twelve o'clock.
— Bellman's verse, 1509

The night before an execution, the bellman was to
stand outside the condemned prisoner's cell and
ring the execution handbell twelve times. In
many towns and villages throughout Europe, the

handbell also rang the next day, along with the Execution Bell, while the prisoner was taken to the place of his death. Some cities even had the name of the executed inscribed on the Execution Bell.

The prisoner also clanged as he walked to his death, as a Convict Bell was hung around his neck. The bell was to remind those seeing the convict to stay on the "straight and narrow," or punishment would await. It was also considered a protective force to keep evil from penetrating any passersby.

The Convict Bell was removed at the gallows or guillotine, but the Execution Bell continued ringing from the church tower. It would be the last sound heard by the convicted person. This gruesome bell rang for the last time in 1890.

THE NINE
TAILORS

When anyone is dying, the bell must be tolled, that the people may put up prayers – twice for a woman, thrice for a man; if for a clergyman, as many times as he had orders – and at the conclusion, a peal on all the bells, to distinguish the quality of the person for whom the people are to put up their prayers.

– Account from 1190

When a person became gravely ill and judged by attendants to be "on their deathbed," the Death Bell was to begin ringing immediately. There were often special bells for this morbid purpose. Many had special mottoes inscribed, such as this verse on an English church bell dated 1608:

All you who hear this mournful sound
Prepare yourselves for underground.

Another from 1701 is short and to the point: *Remember death*. The Death Bell was sometimes referred to as knocks for the dead. When the sober knelling began, fellow villagers were encouraged to pray for the soul of the sick and dying person. It was believed that this ringing also gave comfort to the dying. The poet John Donne wrote about the Death Bell:

And therefore never send to know
for whom the bell tolls. It tolls for thee.

The Passing Bell or the Soul Bell was rung the moment death was imminent. The bell was to accompany the soul on a safe passage, free from evil spirits, as it left the dying body. Over time, a town death was announced by the change in ringing from the church tower. The slow and steady tolling of the bell stopped. At the silence people readied themselves to hear the teller strokes that marked a person's passing. The tellers were referred to as tailors and were rung in sets of three to announce a man's death. Three tolls of the bell and silence, three more tolls and silence, followed by the last of the three tolls – which made for nine teller strokes or nine tailors, meaning a man in the village had died. Hence the expression, "Nine tailors make a man."

A woman's passing was marked by two tolls of the bell repeated three times. For a child it was three long strokes. After the tailors sounded, most villagers would stop their work and strain their ears to count the rings that followed. The church bell would then ring out once for every year the deceased had lived. If, after the nine tailors, there were ninety-nine rings, villagers figured out which of the ninety-nine-year-old men in the village may have passed away.

I measure life: I bewail death.
– English bell inscription

SOUND
THE ALARM

Hear the loud alarum bells,
Brazen bells!
What a tale of terror, now, their turbulency tells!
In the startled ear of night
How they scream out their affright!
Too much horrified to speak,
They can only shriek, shriek,
Out of tune . . .
How they clang, and clash, and roar!
What a horror they outpour
On the bosom of the palpitating air!
        – From "The Bells"
            by Edgar Allan Poe, 1849

The Alarm Bell or tocsin was the warning signal. There was no confusing its insistent and horrid tones with those of any other village bell. Sometimes the tocsin was struck with a large iron rod, over and over again in urgency, or the Alarm Bell might be rung by hammering the clapper furiously against the inside of the bell. However it was sounded, the shrill tocsin sometimes rang for hours on end, creating a great sense of foreboding and emergency throughout the town. One old Alarm Bell cast in Antwerp in 1316 bears a name befitting its purpose. The tocsin is named Horrida.

The tocsin shrieked out impending disaster or invasion. All castles had an Alarm Bell, a tocsin hanging in the turret ready to sound at the first sign of disturbance. To guarantee that the sentries on tower duty stayed awake at their posts, each sentinel was required to ring a small bell on the hour. If the bell did not sound, a superior officer would administer a fit punishment. The castle and kingdom were to be alert for enemy attacks at all times. But the tocsin was also used on occasion by conspirators and murderers in the town as a signal for massacre within.

Whether rung as a warning or to signal an uprising, the piercing, frantic tocsin was a bell citizens wished would remain silent.

Silence that dreadful bell; it frights the isle
From her propriety.
　　　　　– From *Othello* by William Shakespeare

FIRE ALARM
BELL

Lord, quench this furious flame.
Arise, run, help put out the same.
  – Dorsetshire bell inscription, 1652

Fire was greatly dreaded in the Middle Ages. While
the tocsin could sound out an alarm, townspeople
and villagers wanted to react to a fire emergency
immediately. They needed a Fire Alarm Bell whose
sound could not be mistaken for any other. Very often villages would appoint one bell for such purpose. In Coventry,
England the mission of the Fire Alarm Bell at St. Michael's
was inscribed on the bell:

I am, and have been called the Common Bell,
To ring when fire breaks out to tell.

A village might also have devised a special method of ringing the church bells in case of fire. Hearing that peal could mean only one thing – fire. Often the bells were rung backwards. Instead of the traditional descending scale of high bell to low, a fire peal rang from lowest tenor to highest treble bell. In St. Ives, England this reverse ringing rule was inscribed on a bell:

> *When backwards rung we tell of fire,*
> *Think how the world shall thus expire.*

If the fire was in a large town or city, citizens who did not see flames or smoke in their immediate neighborhood waited at their open door to hear the bells following the alarm. The number of bells rung afterward indicated which area of the city was on fire. It might be coded by direction and number of rings, for instance – one for north, two for east, three for south, and four for west.

> *My name is Roelant,*
> *When I toll, that is for fire;*
> *When I chime,*
> *That is for storm in Flanders.*
> — Ghent Alarm Bell inscription

BELLS AND
MORE BELLS

Ronge when any casualtyes chaunce
and for ye gathering together of ye inhabytants.
— In town records, 1552

There were a multitude of occasions requiring bells to be rung in a town. Usually a bell was named according to its municipal duty. Here are some occasional bells.

The Shame Bell or Murder Bell was rung out to call people to the town square to hear a verdict or a pronouncement of justice. It rang until a sizeable crowd had assembled and the court's decision was read. It could be rung to announce a date of execution. In the early days, the bell often rang throughout the course of a duel. One account from 1455 described the disturbing sound of the bell during a duel:

"The big bell, which is hideous to hear, never stopped ringing."

The Tax Bell was also an unpleasant ringing in many people's ears. Its tones summoned people to come to town to pay their taxes. It rang twice weekly from November 11th to Christmas Day. The bell was also called the Tribute Bell and the Tithe Bell.

Just as the Common Bell regulated market hours and affairs of business, the outskirts of town marked activity with the Harvest Bell and the Gleaning Bell.

Each town and city had its own customs concerning its bells. One city rang its Business Bell once every two weeks to remind innkeepers to bring in any bad coins. In some seaports, bells rang when perishable goods and fish were at the dock and needed to be sold immediately.

When a king or queen was pleased or impressed by a certain town or city, a bell was often given as a gift. Bells became symbols of prosperity and royal favor.

> *Prosperity to this town.*
> – Launceston bell inscription, 1720

MORNING BELLS
ARE RINGING

Are you sleeping? Are you sleeping?
Brother John, Brother John,
Morning bells are ringing,
Morning bells are ringing
Ding Dang Dong
Ding Dang Dong.
　　　– From "Frere Jacques"

Monastery life was regulated by the sound of bells throughout the entire day and night. The monks held their first service of the day at midnight. They were woken by the ringing of the Signum Bell in the church tower. While the bell could be heard throughout the whole monastery and probably in the village beyond, there was a second smaller

bell used for the heavy sleepers who hadn't stirred. The Tintinnabulum Bell was rung as a hurry-up call throughout the dormitories. The monks then gathered at midnight for Matins (morning prayer). They stayed in the church for the second service, which followed. The Signum Bell at one o'clock in the morning marked the beginning of Lauds (praise to God). The monks then retired to their sleeping quarters at two o'clock to rest until the next bell.

At seven o'clock in the morning the Signum Bell rang to call monks to a short service called Prime (first). Often they would remain to celebrate Mass. All this before the Nola Bell rang in the refectory to announce breakfast. Bells again called monks to the second Mass at half past eight and to the High Mass at ten o'clock. The small Squilla Bell was up in the choir and rang to mark different parts of the service.

From late morning to after supper, many monks worked in the fields or performed other manual labor. They stopped for dinner at midday, but talking was forbidden then as the Bible was read aloud from the pulpit. Any infractions of rules were punished and the Corrigiunculum Bell was rung sternly before a monk was disciplined. Often a disobedient monk was asked to pray while a lashing was administered.

Then, in the late afternoon or early evening, the Signum Bell sounded again, this time for Vespers (evening worship). An hour was allowed for relaxation before the bell rang again for the final service of the day – Compline (ending). Then the monastery quieted down and the monks went to their dormitories for a few hours of sleep before the Matins Bell announced a new day.

Every day the Signum Bell sounded for at least seven worship services. Two biblical quotations from Psalm 119 laid the foundation for these bell-ringing rules: "Seven times a day do I praise thee," and "At midnight I will rise up and give thanks to thee."

I am the voice of life:
I call you: come and Pray.
   – German bell inscription, Middle Ages

VI

UP IN THE BELFRY: LOFTY PEALS

BELL ROBBERS
FOILED

Horrida Sum Stolidis Latronibus ac Homicidis.
(I am terrible to robber bands and murderers.)
– Ancient bell inscription

The evening the strange occurrence happened began as orderly and uneventfully as any other evening in the monastery. But after the evening service, Compline, just before the monks retired, the Porter Bell at the entrance to the monastery sounded a frantic ringing.

"Who could be ringing at this late hour?" a young novice wondered aloud.

"It must be someone in dire distress," ventured an older monk.

And the novice and the Brother hurried toward the door to see what was causing the tremendous fracas.

They looked out. The agitated face of a man stared back at them through the peephole. "I am in need of your kind assistance tonight, and of course the help of the Lord," said the man. "Pray open the door and give me shelter, for I have nowhere to go at this late hour, and I fear thieves. Pray open the door and let me in."

No sooner had the benevolent Brother and the novice unlocked the door, than they were knocked down by a gang of men, all laughing and jeering. "Learned men you claim to be, but you are really perfect fools," laughed the leader. "Are you daft, then? Have you not heard there are robbers on the road at this time of night? Well, now, my dear monks, you are meeting them in the flesh and bone."

The motley gang of thieves hooted and hollered as they headed for the main sanctuary. They were of a mind to pilfer and destroy. They stuffed goblets, crosses, holy books, and candlesticks into a large woven sack. "There's nothing worthwhile here," cussed one of the rogues, kicking over a row of wooden prayer benches.

The leader shouted to the others: "Well, what say we make merry then, fellows? To the belfry to see what a racket we can raise up there. Who knows, we might even steal those mighty bells of yours, if the spirit strikes us."

The abbot began to pray aloud. "Holy Father" was all he could say before he was interrupted.

"I'll show you what your prayer will get you," yelled the rogues' leader, and struck the abbot so hard across the back that the old monk was dashed headfirst into a pillar. As the monks ran to the aid of their fallen abbot, the robbers rushed to the belfry. They were full of sheer devilment, and laughed and cussed all the way up the steep dark stairway. When they came to the ringing room, each man grabbed a rope and pulled down with all his might. A great clamoring echoed through the church as the robbers rang out their peal.

The monks below fell to their knees at the altar and prayed for swift assistance from divine powers. After an hour of continuous and loud ringing, the monks began to wonder whatever had possessed the thieves to ring for so long. "They must have insane strength to ring so continuously," said the abbot. "Something is not right; let us go to investigate."

The young novice followed at a safe distance behind his Brothers. "God save us all from misfortune this night," he prayed.

The monks made their way up the winding stairway to the belfry. The sight that greeted them there was beyond their wildest imaginings. The robbers looked bewildered, weary, and cross-eyed amidst all the noise. They pleaded, "Help us get down from here!" as they rode up and down on the end of the bell ropes. One screamed, "Please stop this now and we will gladly empty our sack and put everything back in place, neatly. Just tell us what you want and we will do it. Only help end this madness."

"Have you lost your senses, the whole rowdy lot of you?" the abbot said. "For the love of God, simply let go of the ropes."

"Nay, that does not work" was the answer from one of the robbers. "For our hands are stuck fast and we cannot pry them loose, no matter how hard we try."

Faster and faster the bells rang and the robbers flew up and down, as if they were part of some demented dance. They rang a frantic peal for hours on end, then pleaded and begged and wept. But no monk could get near enough to help them, so furious was the ringing.

Come morning, all of the robbers had lost consciousness. And still the bells rang. By noon the bells quieted and the up and down of the ropes came to an end. The old abbot moved gingerly toward the spectacle: the men holding on to their ropes were dead.

"This is the end of that band of robbers," said the abbot deliberately. "They rang themselves to death." At this, the monks all bowed their heads and prayed for the lost souls of the wretches hanging there, still stuck fast to the bell ropes.

This story is based on a curious account published in an 1825 pamphlet on Catholic miracles.

A RIDDLE

Tho' of great age,
I'm kept in a cage,
Having a long tail and one ear:
My mouth it is round,
And when joys do abound,
Oh! Then I sing wonderfully clear.

What am I? The answer is, of course, a bell.
The cage is the steeple, the long tail is the
bell rope, and the ear is the rope wheel
next to the bell.

THE BELFRY
GHOST

A True Story

In mid-May of 1997, Derek Sawyer was up in the belfry of St. James Cathedral in Toronto, performing his duties as tower captain. For years the tower had been empty, but a peal of twelve bells had just been installed and Sawyer was readying everything for their first official ringing on June 27. Satisfied that all was in working order, Sawyer climbed down the tall ladder from the platform above the bells, then closed the belfry door behind him. He began to descend the steep L-shaped wooden stairway that led to the ringing room below. As he came to the turn, he saw a movement out of the corner of one eye and looked down to see what was going on. No one was allowed in the ringing room without his permission, and he had asked his wife, Sue, and her friend to guard the door leading up to the room while he inspected the new bells.

Sawyer looked around. The number four bell rope was swinging back and forth. No windows were open and there was no draft. Besides, none of the other twelve bell ropes was moving. Sawyer was puzzled and his eyes darted about the room looking for the culprit. Then, at the bottom of the stairs, he caught a fleeting glimpse of a man rushing by the number four bell, knocking the rope as he passed. The man then disappeared.

Sawyer raced down the steep stairs to catch up with the intruder. He ran through the ringing room and straight down the staircase to where he knew two persons were standing guard. "Did you see him?" Sawyer panted. His wife and her friend stared blankly at Sawyer, who by this time was exasperated. "How did he manage to slip by the two of you without being seen?" he asked, still looking about for the man.

"No one came down these stairs before you," answered his wife. "In fact, we wondered why you were running down the stairs in the first place."

Now Sawyer was really confused. There was absolutely no other way out of the ringing room except by the staircase. He had seen the man by the ropes, so he had to have run down the stairs to get out, Sawyer told his wife. But she just looked at him calmly and said, "Derek, not only didn't we see this man, but there was only one set of footsteps racing down those stairs, and they belonged to you."

The tower captain was so puzzled that he sat down to think things through. He had seen a man knock the ropes and he saw the number four bell rope swinging in the wake. Then he saw the man dash across the room toward the staircase. And that's when Sawyer realized there was something unusual about the figure. The man in the ringing room was not dressed in modern clothes. He was wearing a high-cut black jacket like a gentleman would have worn in the 1800s.

The event in the ringing room may never be explained, but on the night before the ceremonial dedication and first ringing, Derek Sawyer looked through records kept on the bells. The twelve bells had come from the church of St. James Bermondsey in England, and their first peal had been heard in 1830. When Sawyer looked at the list of those first ringers, one name caught his attention: Edward Sawyer.

Although Derek Sawyer has no firm proof he is related to Edward, he believes it is likely. In fact, he likes to fancy that the man he saw in the belfry that night was his ancestor, Edward Sawyer, hanging around the bells, watching out for them until he was certain they would be looked after properly and rung with care by his descendent Derek.

There is one other possible source for this belfry ghost. The twelve bells now in St. James Cathedral in Toronto are from what is known as a Waterloo church. Because St. James Bermondsey in England was built after the Battle of Waterloo, it is highly likely its bells were made from metal melted down from captured French cannons. The same metal that blasted out war now rings out peace and joy. Who knows what might linger in that metal?

STEEPLE RHYMES

Here is the church and here is the steeple.
Open the doors and see all the people.
  – Nursery rhyme

This old rhyme is a nursery finger play. Wee ones entwine their fingers, put their pointer fingers up together to make a steeple, and open their thumbs like the church doors to reveal all of the congregation – the rest of their fingers. Variations of this old rhyme are heard in parishes all over the British Isles. Some of them were made up by people in neighboring towns, so they are not always the kindest of rhymes.

High church, low steeple,
Dirty town, and proud people.
    – about Dromore and Newry

Little Bowden, poor people,
Leather bells, wooden steeple.
    – about Bowden

The Shalfleet poor and silly people,
Sold their bells to build a steeple.
    – about Shalfleet, Isle of Wight

Boston! Boston!
What hast thou to boast on?
High steeple, proud people,
And shoals that souls are lost on.
    – about Boston, Lincolnshire

Ugly church, ugly steeple,
Ugly parson, ugly people.
    – about Ugly, Essex

A wooden church, a wooden steeple,
Rascally church, rascally people.
    – about Rascall, York

RINGERS' RULES

If to our laws you do consent
Then take a bell, we are content.
— From Ringers' Rules in Flintshire,
England

Ringing has always been serious business and
the rules of the belfry were posted in verse in
most ringing chambers or rope rooms. The
Ringers' Rules covered everything from codes
of behavior and dress to proper ringing and belfry eti-
quette. In many cases, there were punitive rhymes doling
out fines for each ringing infraction. Ringers had to pay for
everything from wearing a hat or spurs to brawling or
cursing in the belfry. The most serious offence and often
the costliest was turning the bell completely over, which

was not only a time-consuming problem to fix but also a dangerous prospect for any of the ringers.

If a ringer pulled too hard on the rope, the bell moved with such force, it would crash through the wooden stay that normally held it in place in its upward or downward position. The bell would then keep on traveling in the direction it was first going, the rope winding so quickly round the wheel, the bell rope below would be pulled straight to the ceiling. Many an inattentive ringer had been pulled off his feet and dashed against the ceiling. The Ringers' Rules posted in 1694 on the belfry wall of All Saints' in Stamford, England reflect the seriousness of turning a bell over.

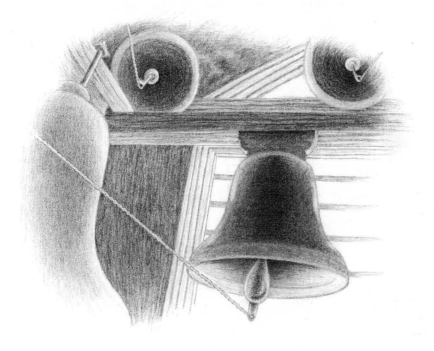

All you that do pretend to Ring
You under take a Dangerous thing
If that a bell you overthrow
Two Pence you pay Before you go.

The Ringers' Rules were stern by design to protect both the bodies and the reputations of bellringers. Despite their serious nature, there was a lot of wit and humor to the verse.

You gentlemen that here wish to ring,
See that these laws you keep in every thing;
Or else be sure you must without delay,
The penalty thereof to the ringers pay.

Next if you do here intend to ring,
With hat or spur, do not touch a string;
For if you do, your forfeit is for that,
Just fourpence down to pay, lose your hat.

But whose doth these orders disobey,
Unto the stocks we will take him straightway;
There to remain until he be willing
To pay his forfeit and the clerk a shilling.

– From rules posted on a belfry wall
in Derbyshire, 1660

In some ringing rooms, a knotted rope called a coult was hung up as a reminder not to break the rules.

If any one these articles
Refuseth to obey,
Let him have nine strokes of the rope,
And so depart away.
Who turns a Bell by light or dark
Two pence shall pay to Parish Clerk.
Who turns a Bell on Sabbath Day
Double the sum at least shall pay.

      – From rules of St. Mary's Church,
      Lincolnshire

RINGING OUT

Those evening bells! Those evening bells!
How many a tale their music tells
Of youth, and home, and that sweet time
When last I heard their soothing chime!
         – From "Evening Bells" by Thomas Moore

A stream of brilliant orange sunlight flooded through the cathedral, glowing like fire on the stone walls and filling the space with a false sense of warmth on a late winter's day. The silence was broken by the creaking of a corner door. An old man walked through, pulling the massive door shut and bolting it behind him. He headed down the center aisle toward the back of the church.

Once there, he opened the door that led to a dimly lit stairwell. The remaining light was now filtered through several thin elongated slits, widely spaced along one side of the stone walls that encased the spiral stairwell. His shoulders touched both walls on the steep climb up. The old man's footsteps thudded and echoed in the stone passageway.

The stairwell ended at a door in the stone wall. This opened to a round room where twelve long ropes hung in a circle. The old man walked by, careful not to set them in motion. The twelve bells above him were "up," as ringers say, and he knew it took very little movement of the ropes to set the heavy monsters above into chaotic swinging.

He had known this for as long as he could remember. His father and grandfather had each been the cathedral's steeple keeper and bell captain before him. With them, he had first climbed up to this ringing room to check on the bells and bid the town good night with a final ring. As a young boy, he learned the bells' names: Margaret, Susanna, Anna Maria, Peter, Old Tom, Bartholomew, Redeemer, Charity, Hope, Grace, John, and Giles. They seemed oddly like family who required regular visits and this he had done faithfully for seventy-five years.

His father taught him a healthy respect for the twelve bells. "Remember, my lad, when the bells are up, the rope is lively," he would always warn. Then would come the story the man had heard from little up, about the poor bellringer who had rung the bells hundreds of years ago in the church. It was a tale with a lesson. "See that number twelve rope over there, son? Well, it's attached to the heaviest bell above us – the tenor." Then his father would bow his head and became very serious. "Now one blustery night, the old bellringer knocked into the rope as he made his way across this very room. And what do you think happened to him?" His father moved in close. "That's right, number twelve rope was lively, boy. It was whipping around in a fury and before that old ringer could think to stand clear, that rope lashed out at him and wrapped not once, but twice, around the poor chap's neck. Next morning the old bloke was found hanging from the end of number twelve in this very ringing chamber."

That old lesson had stuck in his memory. Even though it was many years since he was last told the tale, it came fresh to mind every time he passed by the ropes. He glanced at the wall ahead and assumed the Ringers' Rules posted there had been in place as long as the bells themselves. Every rope room had some version of the rules posted on its wall. They somehow gave a sense of order and safety to events in this ringing world above the village. He remembered when his father had read the first verse of rules to him:

He that in ringing takes delight
And to this place draws near

These articles set in his sight
Must keep if he rings here.

The old man knew the dozens of rules that followed that verse, by heart. He began his ascent into the cathedral's steeple. Above him was a steep and rickety wooden staircase that went up to the ceiling into which the ropes disappeared. The horizon's glow was fading as he mounted the stairs, but the old man didn't mind the disappearing light. His feet had walked these stairs several times a day for decades now and only once, the first time, did he think he couldn't make it. "Keep your eyes on me straight ahead," his father had told him, but being a curious little fellow he looked down to the chamber below. Immediately his knees grew weak and he felt dizzy and hot all over. He gasped and his father turned around just in time to support him. Together they walked down the stairs, which seemed a much harder task than the going-up part had been. "Tomorrow, young lad, we try again," his father had said, "and don't look down." From that day on, he hadn't.

Now he climbed the hundred or more steps without a thought of falling. At the very top, he brought out the keys and fingered the smallest. It unlocked a half-size door that opened inward. He bent over and walked through to near darkness. Startled birds flapped their wings from the rafters above him. The clock below him chimed out six o'clock as he climbed up the narrow metal ladder. It led straight up for another twenty feet to the belfry. At the top he stepped up onto a thin platform, which was really little more than a beam.

He was now high above the bells, looking down into their open mouths. Each bell was housed in its cage with a large grooved wheel around which the rope would wind at each bell stroke. Again his father's stories came to mind – of ringers who had been struck dead when bells had been accidentally rung by someone in the chamber below. He looked down at the two ton tenor bell, the murderous number twelve, beneath him, then over to the innocent and smallest number one – the treble bell down in the far corner.

The old man moved across to the large louvered panels on the side of the steeple, opening them so his evening ring could carry over the whole village. He gazed out far across the wintry town streets, past the fields where only faint echoes of his ringing would be heard. And he thought of the many times the bells had rung out their messages – joyous peals for celebrations and muffled tolling for somber occasions. He and his band of ringers had rung the twelve bells with great determination all night in the year of the spring flood. They rang effortlessly for hours when the war came to an end.

He would soon go down to ring the evening bell and bring a close to the village day. But for a while longer he remained thinking about the times he, his father, and his grandfather had rung the bells. The twelve bells below him had given voice to life in his village, stirring people's souls and filling some with dread. Old stories he had heard about the bells came to mind, and, for just a moment, the old bell-ringer stood still, as if he was straining to hear a sound no one else could hear. For he knew in the air all about him lingered the echoes of all the bells that had ever rung – sounds traveling out to the ends of the world.

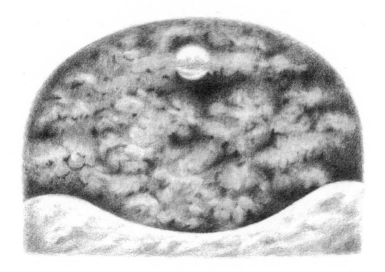

Ring out, wild bells, to the wild sky,
The flying cloud, the frosty light:
The year is dying in the night;
Ring out, wild bells, and let him die.

Ring out the old, ring in the new,
Ring, happy bells, across the snow:
The year is going, let him go;
Ring out the false, ring in the true.

– From "Ring Out, Wild Bells"
in *In Memoriam* by Alfred,
Lord Tennyson, 1850

ACKNOWLEDGMENTS

Thank you to Derek Sawyer, tower captain of St. James Cathedral in Toronto, for allowing me to sit in on a change ringing practice; for sharing his ghost story, ringing rules, and bell tales; and for helping me down the steep belfry steps of St. James. Thanks also to Sue Sawyer, Brigitte Frizzoni at the *Volkskundliches Seminar der Universität Zürich* for answering my questions on European bell superstitions and lore, the late J. Michael Simpson for introducing me to the world of ringing, Sandra Spencer for her musical inspiration, and a ringing round of thanks to my editor, Sue Tate, for the care and all the beautiful touches she brought to these bell stories.

SOURCES

Bassett, Fletcher S. *Legends and Superstitions of the Sea and Sailors, in All Lands and at All Times*. Chicago: Belford, Clarke, 1885.

Briscoe, John Potter. *Curiosities of the Belfry*. London: Hamilton, Adams & Co., 1883.

Hearn, Lafcadio. *Some Chinese Ghosts*. Boston: Roberts Bros., 1887.

Lomax, Benjamin. *Bells and Bellringers*. London: H.J. Infield, 1879.

Morris, Ernest. *Legend o' the Bells: Being a Collection of Legends, Traditions, Folk Tales, Myths, etc., Centered Around the Bells of All Lands*. London: Sampson Low, Marston & Co. Ltd., 1935.

Price, Percival. *Bells and Man*. Oxford: Oxford University Press, 1983.

Raven, J.J. *The Bells of England*. London: Methuen & Co., 1906.

Sayers, Dorothy, L. *The Nine Tailors*. New York: Harcourt, Brace & World, 1934.

Yolen, Jane H. *Ring Out! A Book of Bells*. New York: The Seabury Press, 1974.